PRAISE FOR *THE GUAR*

"A timely work about watching the forces of history roil forth from the confines of one's own home. Sergio Schmucler deftly explores the illusion of control we cultivate in childhood and cling onto through adulthood, and offers the possibility of letting go of it at last. A poignant novel full of grace." — Maria Reva, author of Writers' Trust Fiction Prize finalist *Good Citizens Need Not Fear*

"In Jessie Mendez Sayer's superb translation, *The Guardian of Amsterdam Street* introduces English-language readers to an important and deeply humane writer. Though Sergio Schmucler's short novel elapses within just a few blocks in Mexico City — and then within a few rooms — its scope is large, encompassing history, exile, justice, fate, and love, while featuring seamless cameos by major historical figures. Schmucler's vision, or revision, of a certain Argentinian revolutionary is especially striking and memorable." — Steven Heighton, Governor General's Literary Award–winning author of *The Waking Comes Late* and *Reaching Mithymna*

"This brief, brilliant novel is no more straightforward than the Mexico City street it's named for. If you've ever wandered through the La Condesa neighbourhood, you've likely crossed Amsterdam Street at least several times without meaning to, for it's an ellipse rather than a straight line — you seem to keep meeting it every few blocks. In *The Guardian of Amsterdam Street*, by turns surreal, satirical, allegorical, and deeply engaging, a small boy tries to leave home, but each time he does he ends up where he began. As the novel proceeds with the wonderful illogic of a melancholy fairytale, Amsterdam Street becomes a clock, a history of Mexico, the world, and finally an infinity symbol. We lose ourselves, thoroughly, delightfully, as we learn the elliptical and eventually vertiginous joys and sorrows of a street without end." — Will Aitken, author of Hilary Weston Writers' Trust Prize for Nonfiction finalist *Antigone Undone*

"A deeply human book... Sergio Schmucler achieves a paradox of rare beauty: writing a book about exile that tells the story of someone who has decided not to leave his home." — *La Voz*

"Humour, longing, love, sadness... A study of mankind that Schmucler reveals to the reader in *The Guardian of Amsterdam Street*." — *Arte y Cultura*

The
GUARDIAN
of
AMSTERDAM
STREET

Sergio Schmucler

Translation by Jessie Mendez Sayer

ANANSI
INTERNATIONAL

House of Anansi Press is committed to protecting our natural environment.
This book is made of material from well-managed FSC®-certified forests,
recycled materials, and other controlled sources.

House of Anansi Press is a Global Certified Accessible™ (GCA by Benetech) publisher.
The ebook version of this book meets stringent accessibility standards and
is available to students and readers with print disabilities.

25 24 23 22 21   I 2 3 4 5

Library and Archives Canada Cataloguing in Publication

Title: The guardian of Amsterdam Street / Sergio Schmucler ;
translated by Jessica Mendez Sayer.
Other titles: Guardián de la calle Ámsterdam. English
Names: Schmucler, Sergio, 1959-2019, author. | Sayer, Jessie Mendez, translator.
Description: Translation of: El guardián de la calle Ámsterdam.
Identifiers: Canadiana (print) 20200393332 | Canadiana (ebook) 20200393510 | ISBN
9781487008284 (softcover) | ISBN 9781487008307 (Kindle) | ISBN 9781487008291 (EPUB)
Classification: LCC PQ7298.29.C48 G8313 2021 | DDC 862/.64—dc23

Book design: Jennifer Lum
Cover image: Rand Mcnally and Company. *Mexico Tramways Company: Lines and
properties in Mexico City*. New York: Rand McNally and Company, 1910. Map.
https://www.loc.gov/item/2012593202/.
Interior map credit: Jorge Brozon

*House of Anansi Press respectfully acknowledges that the land on which we operate
is the Traditional Territory of many Nations, including the Anishinabeg, the Wendat,
and the Haudenosaunee. It is also the Treaty Lands of the Mississaugas of the Credit.*

 Canada Council   Conseil des Arts
for the Arts   du Canada

 ONTARIO ARTS COUNCIL
CONSEIL DES ARTS DE L'ONTARIO
an Ontario government agency
un organisme du gouvernement de l'Ontario

*We acknowledge for their financial support of our publishing program
the Canada Council for the Arts, the Ontario Arts Council, and the Government of Canada.*

Printed and bound in Canada

MIX
Paper from
responsible sources
FSC® C103567

The
GUARDIAN
of
AMSTERDAM
STREET

Author's Note

THERE ARE MANY REASONS why Amsterdam Street isn't just any ordinary avenue, the most notorious one being its elliptical shape, as illustrated on the map a few pages ahead.

As far as the name goes, what the official documents say is one thing, and what stands out from reading *Notes on the History of Urbanism* by Carlos Guzmán Elorza, published in 1942, is quite another. An architect whose greatest accomplishment is linked not to his professional feats (the design of only three four-storey buildings in the north of Mexico City are attributed to him) but to the fact that he was a meticulous collector of newspaper columns, articles, and letters written during one of the periods that saw the most urban growth.

Amsterdam Street is located on a piece of land on which the Jockey Club built a racetrack at the beginning of the last century. Every weekend, the city's most glamorous men and women would gather there. Under the shade of the enormous roof that covered the executive box, conversations took place that proved to be very important to the entire country.

For example, on the day of the racetrack's inauguration, the president of Mexico, General Porfirio Díaz, who that day was in full-dress uniform and had groomed his moustache with great care, had the following conversation with one of his most trusted men after seeing the aide arrive looking agitated, his face crumpled in a frown:

"What is it, Pascualito?"

"Forgive the interruption, General, but my friend Gumaro has arrived from his hometown in the north and he brings bad news."

"Go on."

"It appears they are planning an uprising."

"Let them do whatever they want; it won't be the first or the last time we will deal with them. Or have you already forgotten?"

"No, General."

". . ."

". . ."

"The north is a long way away, Pascualito."

"Yes, General, it is a long way away."

". . ."

". . ."

"And when are they planning on launching this uprising?"

"In November, apparently, General. Do you want to know what they have been going around singing?"

"All right, go ahead."

"Yaqui Yaqui Yaqui, it's already raining on the plains, saddle up my trusty horse, I'm with Madero now —"

Just then the racehorses appeared, galloping at full speed towards the finish line, and the spectators' shouts interrupted his song. The general turned to watch them with a look of displeasure.

Apart from being the day he lost more money than anyone else at the new racetrack's first derby, that was the morning when the thorn General Díaz would choke on twelve months later first got stuck in his throat. The revolt that one of his most trusted men told him about ended up becoming a revolution that, with men mounted on hundreds of horses somewhat less elegant than the ones that raced that day on the track, galloped across the country, causing enough turmoil to force him onto a small boat and straight into exile.

Five years later, while the horses of the revolution were still raising clouds of dust in an attempt to prove that the country could have a different destiny and while General Díaz lay dying, plagued by a thousand nightmares in the master bedroom of a house in Paris, those who didn't want to hear about bandits and their desire to create a different country returned to the race-track. This time it was cars they went to see hurtling around the oval track, outfitted with Ford motors and Firestone tires, until, on September 2, 1917, one of them crashed into three curious onlookers who had snuck onto the track, sending the intruders flying into the air with such force that by the time they reached the ground, they were already dead.

In any case, by then so many cars and horses had been around the circuit that their tracks were carved into the ground; something had to be done with them. The architects and engineers who took over the task years later, once Díaz, Pancho Villa, and Emiliano Zapata were firmly in the past, along with the majority of those who used to bet their wealth on the legs of the thorough-breds, decided to turn it into a new business and build thousands of houses using Portland cement. They thought the best thing to do with that racecourse was create a road and build a residential neighbourhood around it that would become the image of the new Mexico, of Modernity and Democracy and Revolution.

The idea was to build a circular road, taking advantage of the south-facing track's curve. But an error in their calculations, and the excessive professional zeal of the project's chief accountant, resulted in Amsterdam Street being built in the shape of an ellipse. Since nobody wanted to admit they would have to modify the blueprints due to an error, the truth was concealed, and they declared that they had planned from the very beginning to use the racetrack as the basis for the new neighbourhood's main avenue.

It was the architect S.E. who proposed the alteration, knowing that a scandal was on the brink of exploding.

A month before the work of building began, the real estate company signed a contract with Zitácuaro Wood LLC in which it was stipulated that the lumber supplier would be paid for its participation in the project with four plots from the first phase of construction and with a house, where their offices would be located. The problem was that the house was built in the middle of the racetrack's oval, slightly too far south, which made it impossible to close the circle of the road without demolishing it.

When the real estate company realized this, they tried to renegotiate with the owner of Zitácuaro, offering him another house instead, but he refused. He knew that if they did not fulfill the terms of the contract the penalty they had agreed upon would work out very much in his favour.

At this point a violent dispute broke out between the person in charge of the project and the accountant, who threatened to quit if they did not honour the agreement, because if they didn't, the debits and credits in his impeccable account ledgers would need to be drastically modified, and he wasn't prepared to let that happen, mainly because that would cast doubt on his reputation, and the resignation of the accountant would have in turn called into question the seriousness of the developer, and that would have cast aspersions on the mayor's entire project, which would have allowed the opposition press to take issue with the Urban Development Plan, which they said had clearly been designed, in their opinion, to favour the private developers, and the matter could have gone as high up as the country's president thanks to the special treatment he gave certain companies, a prime example being the producer of the Portland cement used in these projects, a building product also supported by several opportunistic oil companies that looked favourably upon the expansion of the road networks, and roads require asphalt to allow cars to travel more easily, because easier travel would perhaps result in people buying more cars, so, fortunately for the car companies, oil companies, cement producers, the governors, and the developer, none of this questioning took place because it occurred to the aforementioned architect that he could simply modify the design of the road, respecting the original route of the racetrack, so he stretched the imagined circle into an oval, and in this way avoided demolishing the house where Zitácuaro Wood LLC's offices were located.

In any case, it wasn't the owner of the company from Michoacán who ended up with the house but Mr. Galo Epifanio González, who received it as compensation after he lost a leg at work.

The intricate web of events described here resulted in a humble carpenter becoming the owner of a property in the city's most well-to-do neighbourhood, despite the disapproval of the project's shareholders, who could do nothing to stop it.

The only thing left to mention is the fact that Galo Epifanio González only got to enjoy the house for a little over a year before his death from gangrene. His heir was a nephew who had been his apprentice, and when the nephew grew up he had a son who was named after the uncle, as both thanks and a posthumous tribute to him.

The story told in the following chapters belongs to Galo, the son of the carpenter who inherited the house, and to the elliptical Amsterdam Street.

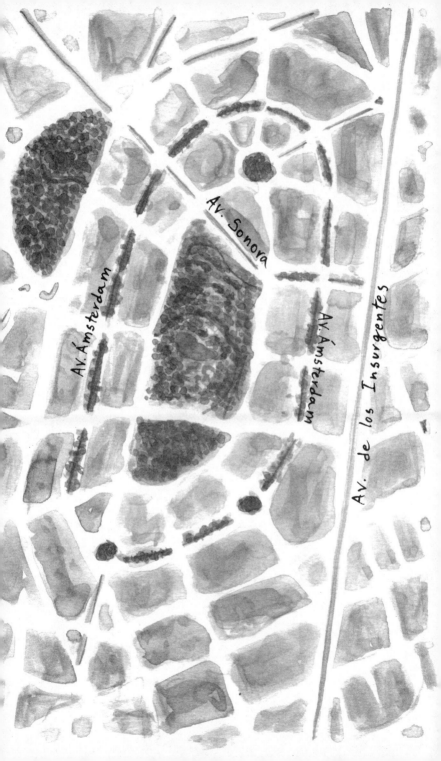

I
=

A BLIND AND DREARY LION is padding along beside his bed.

"Mamá!"

Silence.

A roar. He opens his eyes wide, and again he shouts.

"Mamá!"

But it is his father who appears.

"Your mother will be home in a minute. Go back to sleep while I finish up."

Galo turns over to face the wall and closes his eyes. A moment later the lion roars again: harsh and dreary.

Now he can smell the resin coming from the patio. He sits up in bed so he can see. His father's left knee pushes down on the wood laid across a stack of bricks while his right hand firmly grips a saw that rises and falls and rises and falls, causing the lion to roar, dreary, bored, blinded, and harsh.

Galo sniffs the room. The smell of resin mixes with the kerosene from the cooker that his mother used a little while ago to heat up milk. Outside, on the patio, his father finishes sawing.

Now he is using the brush. Now he is using the coarse sandpaper. Now he is gluing, and nailing with heavy blows of the hammer. Now he shouts to Galo.

"Come to the patio!"

Galo gets up and leaves his room. He goes to his father. He looks at the small chair his father holds in his hands. His father walks to the other end of the patio, where a week ago his mother planted a bougainvillea, and sets the chair down next to it.

"Here you will sit to watch me work. Let's see if you can learn to be a carpenter one day."

For some reason Galo is unaware of, perhaps something to do with the lion that had been threatening him in his sleep, he answers his father like this:

"I don't want to be a carpenter."

The father looks surprised.

"What do you want to be then?"

Galo doesn't answer. Until that moment he didn't know he was supposed to want to be anything.

"You will be a carpenter, or nothing at all," the father says to him as he turns his back to go and wash his body, and Galo sits down in the chair for the first time.

From there he can see the entire patio and the entranceway that leads to the street. He can also see, to his left, the door to the bedroom, where the three of them sleep, and the kitchen. To his right are the two rooms his father uses to store his wood and his tools. Between these rooms and the entrance to the street is the bathroom.

Next to him, the bougainvillea is a dry-looking stick attached to the wall by a delicate string tied to two nails. He and the plant are the same height.

Galo understood that his father was right: He will be a carpenter or nothing at all.

2

=

FROM THAT DAY onwards Galo sits in the chair every morning after drinking a glass of warm milk and eating a torta de tamal prepared by his mother before she leaves for her stand at the market.

His father would have a pastry and some coffee for breakfast. Afterwards he would change from his pyjamas into his work uniform: a white shirt and black trousers. A pencil, a flattened oval red on one end and blue on the other, would be tucked behind his left ear. He always put the orange wooden retractable tape measure in the back pocket of his trousers. In his shirt pocket went the small notebook in which he wrote down the measurements of the furniture he planned to make, a small pack of cigarettes with no filters, and a box of matches.

He was a very tall man, with broad shoulders, and he had a small, well-trimmed moustache, which he made sure never touched the edge of his upper lip.

"If I don't become a carpenter I won't be like him," thought Galo, while his father switched on the radio and waited for the tubes to heat up, and just as Toño Bermúdez's voice came on, his father placed the first piece of wood on the stack of bricks, picked up the saw with his right hand, and began to cut.

For Galo, the war that was starting in Europe smelled like resin, and the tanks and the planes that, according to Toño Bermúdez, were one by one invading the cities and towns of a country called Austria, and then those of another called Czechoslovakia, which Galo hadn't even known existed, sounded like the dreary and harsh roar that covered the floor, and sometimes even filled the air in the patio, with sawdust.

He watched his father's right arm force the saw down and up and down and up, and he remembered that he had once seen in a magazine a man who had the same moustache as his father raise and lower his arm towards and away from the sky as millions of men and women in front of him did the same, and that this was happening in another country with a strange name, while here in Mexico the president also had a moustache, but despite that he was always saying that the man who raised his arm in the magazine was his enemy and he had to be stopped because otherwise the world would end up crushed beneath his boots and tanks and planes, the same ones that were now beginning to fill the air with the smell of resin and with harsh and dreary roars, and the president would say this while Galo's father cut one piece of wood after another, only pausing to smoke a cigarette after the news ended and a man called Carlos Gardel began to sing on the radio.

Once the news bulletin was over, his father would listen to Gardel and seem to become a different person. He would put down the saw and smoke a cigarette, leaning his broad back and the sole of his right foot against the wall, near the bougainvillea and the chair on which sat Galo, who would watch his father and wonder why he always smoked looking up at the sky, and the song on the radio occasionally said, "I return with my brow withered / my temples silvered by time's falling snow."

———

Every morning it was the same. The glass of milk with the tamale sandwich, the father with his coffee and his pastry, then the radio where Toño Bermúdez would say which place the planes were flying towards that day, to drop bombs while the frightened people escaped on bicycles or buses or wagons pulled by horses; and sometimes the bombs and the bullets would hit them, and then the men and the children and the horses would die. But the father hammered and glued and brushed and sanded, leaving the wood smooth, leaving it white and free of splinters, to make chairs, tables, beds, bookshelves, and wardrobes, and he would wipe the sweat off his face with a rag that became greyer and wetter by the minute, and then he would lean against the wall and smoke and listen to the songs that Gardel sang, looking up at the sky.

———

Galo learned in those days that for the world to be as it was, it was necessary for men to have moustaches.

One raised and lowered his arm and sent tanks and planes all over the place. Another said that oil belonged to the Mexican people and would turn Mexico into a great country. And the other, the one Galo had to watch extremely carefully from his chair, built furniture so that people could sit or lie down or put their clothes away while the war was far away, and in the houses on Amsterdam Street there was still no need to build shelters to protect people from the bullets and the bombs and the gas that wanted to begin combining with the smell of resin and sawdust in Europe. All of this meant Galo could relax: the three men did what they needed to do to make sure he could remain in his chair, next to the bougainvillea.

=====

When the father finished working he would put his tools away in a trunk. Then he would arrange the finished furniture, or the pieces that were not yet finished, in the rooms next to the entrance to the house, and he would get into the shower to wash his body. He always washed in the same order: first his right arm, then his left, then his neck, and finally his face, swirling a little bit of water around in his mouth, which, as he vigorously scrubbed his cheeks and his closed eyes, he would then spit out in a high-pressure spurt. Galo watched from his chair because he was determined to learn how to be a carpenter, and in order to be one he also needed to know how his father washed his body. A moment later, once he finished drying himself off, the father would walk across the patio and into the kitchen where the mother served him food and told him what had happened at her stall at the market. Galo sat in his chair, ate in silence, and listened. Later, in the afternoon, the mother would sweep the sawdust and water the bougainvillea, and the father would leave the house wearing another shirt and a different pair of trousers, which had no glue or the smell of resin on it, and would return only after Galo had already fallen asleep.

3
=

ALL OF THESE THINGS happened over and over again for the first six months after Galo started sitting in the chair. But one day something occurred that would change his life entirely: along with the red-and-blue pencil, the notebook, and the orange wooden measuring tape, the father, after drinking his coffee and eating his pastry, also placed a black plastic comb in the previously empty back pocket of his trousers.

The previous day the following events had taken place: at the moment Gardel had begun to sing, and the father was already resting his back and the sole of his right foot against the wall and had lit his cigarette with no filter and begun looking seriously and pensively at the sky, a woman walked onto the patio.

She was very different to his mother. She had long, wavy blonde hair that covered almost half her face. She was as tall as his father. Her lips were red, and she walked as if her feet had no need of the floor. She wore a blue silk dress and a white pearl necklace.

"Good morning, I want to place an order."

Galo watched as his father's gaze came down from the sky to meet hers, and found two burning blue embers.

"I need a trunk made."

For a moment, Galo thought his father's body had disappeared into the woman's blue eyes, meanwhile Gardel's voice on the radio was saying, "She came back one night / I wasn't expecting her / so much worry on her face."

Drawing deeply on his cigarette as if wanting, Galo thought, the smoke to release him from the prison of those eyes, he tilted his head towards the door leading to the furniture-making rooms.

"Come this way."

"She told me meekly / 'If you forgive me, it could be like the old times,'" Gardel continued, while the father and the woman went into the largest room and stopped in front of the tool trunk.

From his chair, Galo could see two tall shadows outlined by the light coming in through the window that faced the street. They talked for a moment, and then the woman leaned forwards slightly and ran her hand across the top of the trunk, as if she had yearned to caress it.

They came back onto the patio. The woman smiled with an expression that Galo thought looked like sadness, and the father asked her when she needed the trunk by.

"As soon as possible, I have to go back to my country within a week."

He realized that, in that instant, his father felt a strong pain somewhere in his body, and that he tried to hide it, but that somehow the woman had noticed and, looking down for a moment, she explained. "I work for a company that is leaving Mexico permanently."

As she finished saying the word *permanently,* she tucked her hair behind her ear with the hand she had used to caress the trunk, but almost immediately it fell across her face again and covered her right eye, and then his father's right hand, as gently as it had always slid across recently sanded wood to check its smoothness, and that would, at times, tightly grip the saw, rose into the air and gathered the fallen hair. The hand, Galo thought, had risen and crossed the space between their bodies to try and tuck the hair back into place because it wanted to make sure the father could keep looking at those eyes, and the unexpected movement of the hand allowed both of them to look at one another for three more seconds without saying anything, and then she left, and her feet seemed to float in the air, and Galo's father followed those steps and that body that was moving farther and farther away with the same look he gave the sky each morning while he smoked and leaned against the wall.

The father picked up the saw with both hands. He held it against his chest, closed his eyes, and listened to the last verse of the song on the radio.

4

T HE FOLLOWING MORNING Galo's father put the black
plastic comb in his pocket, the comb that would change
the course of history.

The day began almost the same as all the others before it,
but now, while the presenter Toño Bermúdez was saying goodbye, instead of lighting a cigarette, the father took out the comb
and pulled it slowly through his hair, six times in a row. He did
something else he had never done before: just after the adver-
tisements had finished and as Gardel was about to start singing,
instead of leaning against the wall and smoking and looking up
at the sky like always, he fixed his gaze upon the entrance to the
house, and his eyes looked towards the door as though waiting
for something they already knew was going to happen, as if they
were convinced they were already looking at what they would
see a moment later, or, Galo thought, as if looking at it that way,
they could will what they wanted to happen there into being.

The door opened and the woman walked in.

They said nothing. They looked at one another the same
way they had the day before. The woman took a few steps forwards, and once she was in the middle of the patio, next to the
wood on the pile of bricks, the father walked over and stopped

in front of her. It seemed to Galo that they were so close to one another that if, in that moment, they had wanted to separate they would not have been able to tell to whom each nose or pair of lungs belonged.

Just then, he circled her waist with the same hand that he would run gently across a recently sanded piece of wood, that would move the saw to make it rise and fall harshly, and he pulled her towards his body; now it was not just their breath that was mingling but also their stomachs and chests.

They started to spin and fuse the parts of their bodies that had remained separate: their legs, heads, fingers, waists. Now it wasn't only the lady's feet that seemed to make the ground look unnecessary, because the father's feet were floating too.

When there was nothing left of them that had not fused, when their bodies seemed to cease being their bodies and began to look like a spinning top, just when Carlos Gardel was about to finish singing and when Galo thought he had finally understood why his father leaned back every day against the wall to smoke and look up at the sky, in the exact moment when the sky came down and entered the eyes of that woman, enabling Galo to see it up close, his mother entered the patio, feet firmly on the ground, holding the bag she had brought from the market to prepare lunch . . . then Galo discovered that his mother had roars hidden in her throat as loud as those of the tanks and the planes, and that those roars were capable of filling the air with more sawdust, gas, bombs, and bullets than all the armies that were, at that moment, beginning to devastate Europe, because she let the bag filled with potatoes and sweetcorn and chilies fall to the ground, and she picked up the saw.

She didn't care that Carlos Gardel had not yet finished singing the final verse of his song, nor that she had heard at the market that President Lázaro Cárdenas was, that very afternoon, going to take the oil away from the foreigners, and that any Mexican who loved their country should go to the centre of the city to support him, nor that her son was watching everything from his chair because he had to learn to be a carpenter or he would be nothing at all, and mistaking the lady's right arm for a piece of wood filled with resin, she sawed through her wrist.

5
=

"MY HAND, BRING MY HAND!"

The lady screamed as though she was one of those women fleeing the towns and the cities so that the bombs wouldn't hit them, and Galo, still and silent, gazed at the hand that had just yesterday delicately caressed the tool chest and that was now lying on the ground next to the bougainvillea, covered in sawdust and blood.

The woman screamed as she ran towards the street, leaving a red trail behind her, and Galo's father picked up the hand, sawdust and all, and followed her out.

The mother went into the bedroom to shout and cry, and she did not stop until her husband returned, ten hours later. He told her he was leaving, that she would never see him again. She tried to stop him by telling him to stay, not for her sake, but for his son.

Galo listened to his parents from the chair, since, after everything that had happened, he preferred to remain seated and wait. He had only risen three times during the ten hours his father was out: once to go to the toilet to pee and the other two times to see if his mother was alive, because twice she had stopped crying, and since she had taken the saw with her it occurred to him that, just as she had cut off the lady's hand, she might also have cut off her own head.

"If you want, I will take him with me," the father said to the mother, "but I never want to see you again."

The mother knew that if she allowed him to take the child she would be left with nothing.

"My son will never leave this house. Certainly not to go off with that American whore."

The father came out onto the patio, stood before Galo, looked at him for a moment, and then left.

Galo would next see his father forty-three years later.

6

=

T HE FATHER HAD MADE Galo a chair so that he would sit
and watch him. He told him: "You will be a carpenter or
nothing at all," and then he left, almost forever.

The mother threw out the tools and all the carpentry materials three hours after uttering the words, "My son will never
leave this house."

The oil now belonged to Mexico; Austria, Czechoslovakia,
and Poland belonged to the Germans.

Toño Bermúdez kept on reading the morning news bulletin,
and Carlos Gardel kept on singing.

Galo turned seven years old, and he had a mother, a bougainvillea, a chair, and two big dilemmas to resolve: Would he
leave the house, and how would he learn to be nothing at all.

He had no idea where to begin, because up until that
moment he had left all the decisions to the three men with
moustaches. But they had failed him, and he could no longer
trust them. If it hadn't been for the bombs and the tanks of one
(as he had heard on the news), another wouldn't have dared to
take the oil; if he hadn't taken the oil, the woman with the blue
eyes wouldn't have left the country; if she hadn't left the country, she wouldn't have needed a trunk, and therefore wouldn't

have met his father, who would therefore still be looking up at the sky while smoking and cutting planks of wood, and Galo would be as he had been for so long, sitting in the chair, trying to learn how to be a carpenter, and his mother wouldn't have said that he would never leave the house.

"I will learn how to be nothing at all," he thought, "but to know whether or not I should listen to my mother, I should first see what's out there."

He decided to see the world, so he opened the door that led to the street.

7

=

WHEN HE CLOSED the door behind him, his mind filled with doubts, Galo decided to walk along Amsterdam Street, in one direction, to see what there was to see and, above all, where it would take him, because before Carlos Gardel started to sing that morning, he had recited a prologue that went . . .

Young man, listen to this song,
which was written in pain.
It is simply the advice
of someone already lost.
When life takes you away
from home without reason,
kid, make no mistake!
Don't let hope fool you:
It's not the treacherous knife
that makes the streets so dangerous,
but how far from home hope leads
your sad heart.

===

He saw trees, cars, houses, men with and without moustaches, women stuck to the ground and others who floated. He saw children who looked like him, he saw dogs, and he saw cats. He saw a hunched man dressed in rags. Another wearing a cape that was red on the inside and black on the outside. Another smoking with his eyes closed. Another who splashed water on the bakery window and then wiped it with a cloth.

He kept walking, and on one corner there was a magazine stand, and he spotted a newspaper with photographs of the man from Germany as well as airplanes and tanks. He saw photographs of President Lázaro Cárdenas and a drawing of an oil well.

On another corner he noticed a man watching a woman in the same way his father had observed the sky going inside those two blue burning embers.

And he kept going farther and farther. At every street that crossed the one he was walking along he saw bicycles and trucks, and up ahead he saw windows, some closed and others open, allowing him to see inside houses, some of which looked like his and others that did not.

And he saw a roundabout with a fountain at its centre, and he saw two girls licking a chocolate ice cream cone at the same time, and he saw a policeman talking to another policeman. And he saw a woman using her broom to push a small mouse, its head squashed, to the edge of the sidewalk.

Galo walked and walked along Amsterdam Street, until he suddenly found himself in front of his own front door.

And so in he went, and he sat down on his chair next to the bougainvillea and thought: "I have seen windows and dogs and children like me; I've seen bicycles and trucks, but if the street brought me back here again, it doesn't make any sense to leave again. My mother was right." And thinking this, he learned something that would prove very important for him in the future: just as things leave, they must also return.

And this is how on December 7, 1939, at four o'clock in the afternoon, Galo, who had been left without a father, who had a bougainvillea to look after and a chair upon which to sit, realized that his life would take place inside that house.

8

"**I**'M WORRIED ABOUT my son. I have tried to get him out of the house, but it's impossible. It's been over a month since he last left. Yesterday I tried to force him out, but he threw himself to the ground and I don't know what happened, but it was as if he had fainted; his eyes were closed and he wasn't moving. When I picked him up and took him back inside, he woke up, and since I thought he was just being a little brat, I gave him a smack on the bottom and dragged him outside onto the street again, and that's when he fainted for the second time."

"Bring him to me for a checkup."

"But I already told you, I cannot get him to leave."

"All right," the doctor said. "I will come and see him tomorrow afternoon."

The doctor prodded Galo's stomach, looked at his throat and his ears, took his temperature, and decided that he had no illness that was stopping him from leaving the house, and then Galo told his mother that even if he was not ill, even if there was

nothing wrong with his stomach or throat or ears that the doctor needed to cure, he couldn't leave because the street would
just bring him back to the house again.

His mother asked the doctor what she should do, and the
doctor told her to wait, that she shouldn't pressure him because
she might make it worse, but that if, after a while, nothing had
changed she must take him to see a mental specialist, because
there was probably something wrong with him.

At first the mother was scared. Then, following the advice of
a customer, she went to ask Matilda, the lady to whom God had
given the power of healing, and Matilda told her that there was
something wrong with her son's head because of something he
had seen when he was younger, and the mother remembered
that Galo had seen her saw off her husband's lover's hand, and
she thought that must have been it.

"A child who has experienced a great shock is just like a
slow-witted child," Matilda told her. "There's nothing to be
done. You must get used to your son the way he is."

And so the mother saw him as slow-witted, and never again
did she want to force him to leave. She became used to seeing
him sitting in his chair next to the bougainvillea, or listening to
the radio, and decided she would not send him to school, and
after a while she said: "It's all right, but if you don't want to
leave the house you must be useful inside it," so she taught him
how to carry out domestic chores, which was how Galo learned
to cook, clean the windows, wash the laundry, and water the
plants; and the moment he learned how to do all of this his
mother made a new decision that would once again change his
life, just like when his father had slipped a black plastic comb
into his back pocket: she put up a sign on the street that read
"Two rooms for rent."

9
=

H<small>E WAS A PALE MAN</small>, with a beard. He took off his hat, and as he twirled the rim between his fingers he glanced around the patio.

The mother asked how many of them there were. The man told her three: his father-in-law, his daughter, and himself, but when he spoke he didn't sound like anybody else. Galo thought his words were strange, as if they hung from his mouth by threads that were permanently tangled between his teeth.

"All right then, you can stay," said the mother, and she went to open the doors of the rooms that a year ago were occupied by the carpentry workshop.

Galo was sitting next to the bougainvillea, watching, and a moment later the man appeared in the doorway of one of the rooms and told the mother that he liked them very much but there were no beds or furniture. She told him that the rooms were to be rented as they were. The man went out onto the street. The mother came over to Galo and told him to take a cloth and wipe down the floor of the smallest bedroom because it was covered in dust. Galo went to find the cloth and a bucket of water, and when he came back across the patio and walked past the open door, he glimpsed an old man and a girl getting out of a black car. Meanwhile, the man was lifting a large green metal chest from the trunk of the car which, with the help of the girl, he quickly put down in the entrance.

A moment later the three of them stood in the entrance to the patio with the chest in front of them. The mother closed the door and told the man that as soon as they had gotten themselves settled he was to come and see her in the kitchen — which from then on would also be the administration office for the rented rooms — so they could settle the question of the price as well as other formalities.

Galo thought the girl was beautiful. Her eyes were green, and her hair was curly, the colour of a dark varnish he had seen his father use on the softer woods.

He approached the door of the bigger room and heard words he did not understand. He watched them moving their lips but he could not comprehend what they were saying. The man eventually began to stroke the girl's hair, and the old man dropped down onto the chest, using it as a chair. The girl noticed Galo spying on them and went out onto the patio. Standing next to her, he noticed the difference in height between them: the girl was at least a head taller than he was.

"Did you understand?"

"No."

"We speak German. It's another language."

"But you speak Spanish just fine."

"Yes, I do. My grandfather does too because he learned it when he was young, but he doesn't want to say anything, and my father only knows a few words. What's your name?"

"Galo."

"I'm Ana."

They went silent because the man appeared and walked across the patio and into the kitchen, where the mother was waiting for him.

"Why doesn't your grandfather want to speak?"

"Because he is going to die, and when someone is going to die they don't want to speak anymore. You'd best not go near him. My grandfather is crazy, and he could hit you."

Galo looked at the old man through the room's window. He was still sitting on top of the chest, looking intently at his shoes. Galo thought it looked as though he had tears in his eyes. Galo couldn't keep talking to Ana because the father had now appeared in the kitchen doorway, calling for her.

"Ana, my child, come and help me." The man had asked Ana to come to the kitchen so that he and the mother could talk easier.

"My father would like to know," the girl said, "where he can go to buy beds and a few pieces of furniture."

"There's a furniture store right next to the market," Galo's mother said, before adding with unexpected generosity, "I have some time now. If you'd like I could come with you."

Ana's father thanked her with a gesture and the two of them went out onto the street.

And now Ana looked around the house. She went into Galo's and his mother's room; she went into the kitchen and then the bathroom, with Galo always trailing behind her.

"My house in Berlin was much nicer than this one."

"Why did you come here?"

"Because of the war. Because they want to kill us."

"Why?"

"Because we are murderers. We were the ones who killed Christ."

Above his mother's bed was a crucifix. Ana went right up to it and explained to Galo.

"We nailed his feet and his hands to the cross so that he couldn't move. We left him hanging there for three days without anything to eat or drink and he died."

"You did that?"

"Not me, but my ancestors did."

"Why?"

"Because he didn't want to follow God's law and anyone who doesn't want to follow God's law must be killed."

"Was that the rule in your house in Berlin?"

"Uh-huh, so if you don't want the same thing to happen to you, you have to do everything I ask."

"What will you ask me to do?"

"I don't know, I'll think of something, and if you tell your mother it won't go well for you. Do you know how to smoke?"

"No."

"Come, I'm going to teach you. But not here. Where can we hide?"

Galo didn't know where to hide, but Ana came up with the idea of going up to the roof. He had never been up there, and he marvelled at the view. In the distance, above the tops of the ash trees on Amsterdam Street, he could see the castle on top of Chapultepec Hill. To the south was Ajusco mountain, and behind it, the volcanoes. While Galo looked at the city and the mountains that surrounded it for the first time, Ana lit a cigarette with her eyes closed, as though she didn't care at all about what they could see.

"They taught me how to smoke on the boat. I really like it. My mother smoked like this," Ana said, holding the cigarette as though it had a long filter, and when she blew out the smoke her lips were stretched forwards in a *u*, and when it reached Galo's face it was in the shape of small doughnuts.

"Where is your mother?"

"She's dead. Here, it's your turn."

Galo couldn't do it because as soon as he felt the hot smoke in his throat he began to cough.

"You'll learn."

"Will you be staying in my house for a long time?"

"I don't know. And your father? Doesn't he live with you?"

"No. He went to live in another country."

"Just like us," Ana said.

IO

T HE MAN BOUGHT three single beds, a chest of drawers for their clothes, a table, sheets, and some blankets and pillows. The following day he came back with a lamp and some books, which, Galo overheard, had been given to him for Ana at a place called Mount Sinai Beneficence. She needed to study if she was to start school. Two days later some friends found the man a job in a butcher shop that belonged to a man named Burakov, and where he had to arrive early in the morning and stay until late. And so, in less than a week after arriving at the house, he had managed to establish a routine for himself and his daughter.

As the days passed, Galo noticed a change in his mother's temperament; he even heard her singing as she made the bed on some mornings, something she hadn't done since his father had left. She started coming home a little earlier from the market to make sure the house was cleaner than before. He noticed that every night, a few minutes before the man was due to return from his work, she would become nervous, look at herself in the mirror, and powder her nose, and she would tell Galo to set the table in the kitchen so that they could all sit together to eat the cold cuts and chunks of sour fish that the man brought home with him — all except Ana's grandfather, who was hardly ever hungry and always stayed in the smallest room, with the door firmly shut.

As well as spending her mornings studying, Ana joined in with the kids who met up every afternoon in Parque México. When she got bored of studying or came back from the park looking angry, she would go up to the rooftop to smoke; sometimes she would make Galo go with her, and other times, even if he wanted to join her, she wouldn't allow him and would go up there alone.

===

One afternoon the old man came out of his room dragging a sheet behind him and went into the bathroom. Galo didn't see him; instead he was intently observing how the bougainvillea had grown sprouts that would become its first flowers. But a moment later he heard strange noises coming from the bathroom and went to investigate.

The door was half open, and he could see Ana's grandfather standing on the toilet with one end of a bedsheet wrapped around his neck. He was attempting to tie the other end around the shower pipe. Once he managed this, he let himself fall and his body swung through the air, twenty centimetres above the ground. Galo watched him as the man swung and stretched out his legs as though he were kicking an attacker that Galo could not see. So hard did he fight his invisible opponent that the sheet came loose and he fell to the floor, gasping for breath, coughing, his whole face very red, and he began to vomit. Afterwards he sat down on the toilet and used the sheet to wipe his face clean.

II
===

"THERE NEVER HAS BEEN nor will there ever be a perfume factory like mine. No one will be able to create a concentrate like the one we made, and I don't say so just for the sake of it, I say so because the whole world knows it . . . and when the whole world knows something it's because that's the way it is.

"This is what I wanted to explain to Franz, but Franz always was and always will be a fool, a spoiled child. He showed me that piece of paper covered in stamps and signatures he had gripped in his hand as he ran all the way from the Administration and Commerce Office to the factory, as if it wasn't a piece of paper at all but a flag flapping in the wind. He told me: 'Mr. Gueiser, you must hand over the factory to me this afternoon,' and I replied: 'You and all the idiots who signed that piece of paper can go to straight to hell and wipe your asses with it!' But Franz wasn't at all troubled, in fact I had never seen him so relaxed. 'I did not create the law, and besides I have nothing against you.' 'Then go and tell them not to take the factory away from me!' And then he did the most repugnant thing he could have possibly done: he glanced down at his left foot for a moment, and then, without looking me in the eye, he said: 'I cannot do that, you know I cannot.'

"The most absurd thing of all is that Franz knew that in the seven years he had been working as my assistant in the factory, he hadn't learned enough to continue producing the perfumes to the same standard of quality that I had always maintained or that any son or grandson of mine would have upheld, because creating perfume is something you have in your blood; you have to know certain things that you cannot learn in any school, not even by watching an old man doing it for seven years. You can add the same amount of essences, you can mix them the same number of times, you can add the alcohol and the fixative just at the right moment, but it will never come out the same. Don't ask me why, but that's just the way it is and always will be. Even for the last Pesach we spent at home, my wife, may she rest in peace, invited him to dinner with us because she thought of him as part of the family. . . . But the truth is the truth, and as much as we refused to see it, it was still the truth: Franz was always German, and although we lived amongst them and worked for them and they worked for us and we got married and we got divorced and nobody spoke of God or anything of the sort, except for during the festivals, the Jews never stopped being Jews. And so they celebrated their Christmas and they invited us to eat roast duck and sausages and we celebrated Yom Kippur and Rosh Hasha-nah and we invited them over to eat kamish broit and matzo balls, and after Christmas and after Yom Kippur their children and ours would go out together and dance at the same parties organized for young Christians and young Jews, and they stud-ied in the same school and they fell in love with the same girls . . . until that devil arrived who drove them mad and told them we were worse than the plague and Lenin, and that we were deformed, and that we had stolen their factories and their cloth-ing shops, and that we smell terrible; then they stopped inviting

us to Christmas and they stopped coming to our houses, and
from one day to the next they stopped our children from going
to the same schools as their children, and the hairdressers started
putting signs in the windows saying 'We only cut German hair,'
and in the bookshops they stopped selling books in Yiddish. . . .
But I didn't care about that. It will pass, I said, and I kept making
perfumes and I kept selling them to the same people that had
been buying them from me for years, and I never told Franz that
he could no longer be my assistant, not even on the day that he
came to show off his Hitler Youth uniform . . . until he came
running with that stupid piece of paper, filled with signatures
and stamps, as if it were a flag, which said that, according to
the expropriation decree number such-and-such, the manage-
ment of the Joseph Gueiser and Sons Perfume Factory should
be transferred that very afternoon to Mr. Franz Weill, assistant
to the general director and owner, the Jew Samuel Gueiser.

"'I assure you that I won't allow anything to change, Mr.
Gueiser, you will keep living in the house, and I will continue
to be your employee, but the paperwork must be different, and
you must understand how things are now, you and all your race,
you can never again be the owner of any factory in Germany;
but it isn't my fault, and anyway it's better this way, that I stay
in charge, because imagine if you refuse, then the Administration and Commerce Office will take it all away from you, and
they will hand it over to god knows who, someone who knows
nothing about your perfumes.' You know what I did after he
said that? I locked myself in the office toilet and I cried, yes, I
cried for three hours and twenty minutes, because I had sworn
it would never happen to me, not to us, that they might do it to
the Jews who isolate themselves, always speaking in Yiddish and
looking down on the Germans, but not to me, the man who

went every Friday to Mr. Roik's pub to get drunk and sing along to the war songs with everybody else, and who never stopped working with the board at his granddaughter Ana's school . . . not to me, the man who always felt more German than any of those miserable wretches, the same ones who only a few years earlier had been too cowardly to face the French and had run away, terrified, towards the woods and hid behind the birch and cypress trees until a Red Cross truck passed by with white flags flying . . . but after crying for three hours and twenty minutes I made a decision: it's all right, I thought, I will hand over the factory facilities and the essences to Franz, but first I will hide the Love perfume concentrate under my bed, I will not give them that. And so I hid the three-litre bottle of concentrate under my bed and left it there, because as long as I had that I would be able to start over again, no matter where, or when . . . one day I would set up my perfume factory anew, and those idiotic Nazis wouldn't get the better of me, of Samuel Gueiser, son and grandson of the best perfume manufacturers on Kinkel Street and in all of Berlin!

"The day arrived when my son-in-law decided it was time to leave. Ana could no longer go to school. 'We cannot take everything from the house,' he told me, 'just pack what is most essential and leave everything else behind.'

"I waited for him to finish putting the chest into the taxi, and then I came out with my bottle wrapped in a black jacket so that nobody would see it, because on the pavement in front of the factory office and the entrance to the house that had belonged to my family for more than a hundred years were all the goyim neighbours from the block, and they watched us with serious expressions, and some of them, like Mrs. Hubermas, were smiling, and others, like Mr. Schnidzer, lowered their gaze, and my poor little Ana and her father walked to the taxi as if they were naked, because those smiles and those lowered gazes seemed like knives slashing at their clothes; but not me, I walked with my head held high, firm, proud, with my bottle hidden under its black disguise. Franz came out of the factory office to say goodbye. My son-in-law and Ana shook his hand, but I only looked at him with scorn and said, 'Rot in hell, Franz,' and we got into the taxi, and not one of the Kinkel Street residents opened their mouths to say a word, and we left as quickly as we could. In the rear-view mirror I could see how some of them began to embrace Franz, while in the taxi my son-in-law embraced his daughter, who had started to cry, because she had just realized she had forgotten to pack her most cherished doll inside the chest.

"We were able to leave the city without any serious problems. We were luckier than the Feldmans, who, as they were leaving through the north of the city, were stopped and had their passports confiscated, and they were kept for three days in a room without electricity and without a toilet, to then be told that it had been a mistake and they could continue on their way. The German police watched us cross the checkpoint between the last street in the city and the highway in silence, but I knew that they were happy to see us leave, and I spat on the ground of the city that I so loved, and I didn't turn back to see how one by one the streets disappeared in the distance, along with the days and months and years of my life.

"The only thing I could think about in that moment was how I would re-establish the factory with my Love concentrate and how I would laugh in the faces of those mediocre men and women and show them that, no matter what they did, they would never be able to defeat me.

"We got to Hanover where we had to change trains. It took four days for us to get to Basel-Stadt, after crossing the whole country from north to south. Looking out of the train windows we saw Jews of all kinds: tall, thin, fat, feeble, rich ones in their cars, and poor ones in their horse-drawn carts, and goyishe peasants on the outskirts of dozens of towns who watched them all moving along, shrouded in dust, the way someone might watch a grazing cow with indifference. In this last Swiss city, we boarded a train with a French flag which took us to Paris, and from Paris we took another to Cannes. My poor Ana was tired. I, on the other hand, enjoyed those days of travel because I was getting farther away from Kinkel Street, and because I thought I was getting closer with every passing day to starting anew. My enormous bottle and I.

"My son-in-law looked into how we could find a boat that would take us to Argentina; I was keen to head there because my older sister and two of my nephews had already gone to that southern country, but the only boat sailing from the port of Cannes in the next few days was heading to Mexico.

"'As soon as I get there I will start up the Gueiser perfume factory again,' I told myself every single day of the journey, as the ship's prow split the ocean's waters in two . . . but when we disembarked at the port, when I could almost taste my vengeance, I tripped and the bottle slipped from my hands.

"Just like in the story of the little girl who walks along a forest path with her jug of milk, thinking about everything she will do with the money once she sells it at the market, I dropped the barrel of Love concentrate. The air became perfume; for a few minutes the seawater was no longer salty because it was steeped in concentrate. Imagine the smell, if just three drops are enough to make half a litre of perfume. The sailors of the

Crozatier did not see what had happened and were surprised: they had never arrived at a port that smelled so pleasant, and I sat down on the stairway in a state of shock for I don't know how long, because that was when I realized that the Gueiser perfume factory would never again exist, and that my family, along with my ancestors and Berlin and Kinkel Street and all the world's Jews were lost to the devil, and this is what I realized just before I stepped down onto the port of Veracruz for the first time . . . may the heavens open and let vomit rain down upon it.

"This is why we are here, but as far as I am concerned we could be anywhere . . . we could have stayed in Veracruz, or still be on board the ship, or on Kinkel Street so that the Nazis could taunt and murder us, stupid Jews, useless scourge, miserable children of a God who abandoned them. I don't care about Mexico, I don't care about this house, I don't care about you, Galo, even though you have become such a good friend to Ana and you just saw me attempting to die."

"Mr. Gueiser? Argentina, the place you want to go. Is that where Carlos Gardel lives?" Galo asked.

"Gardel is dead, you stupid kid," he said, and walked out of the bathroom, dragging the sheet behind him.

12

"MY MOTHER DIED of a very rare disease, so rare they wouldn't let me see her once she was dead because they feared I would catch it. They told me her body was covered in sores and that she screamed as though she were burning in hell. That's why I couldn't even go and visit her grave; they closed the cemetery so nobody would catch that disease ever again.

"I loved her very much. I don't love my grandfather, because he is crazy. When we lived in my house the only thing he did was mix smells. That's what he did for a living. He spent all his time sniffing jars to see if the concentrates were properly concentrated or if he needed to wait a little longer to mix them. Nobody who spends their life smelling things can be intelligent. The sense of smell is for animals, for dogs who are always smelling their own bottoms or where another dog just peed . . . and besides at the back of my house there was a cage with rabbits inside that would eat and have babies and pee, and my grandfather got his helpers to collect the rabbit pee and would use that too for his disgusting perfumes . . . that's why when I had boogers I didn't like to pick them, so that my nose would stay blocked and I didn't have to smell anything at all.

"In the afternoons, when my mother would get back from the shop, we would go into her bedroom and shut the door and dress up. I would put on her silk stockings and her white shoes with bows on them and she would mess up my hair and afterwards get me to try on all her hats in front of her closet mirror, but I would always end up wearing the black one with two blue feathers on the side, and while we pretended to be friends drinking tea together we listened to her favourite records and danced, me in the black hat and the white shoes, her wrapped in long bits of silk fabric she had bought from a lady who brought them from India. When they took her to hospital I kept locking myself in her room and dressing up in front of the mirror. I asked my father if he would let me put some of those clothes in the chest, but he said no. Instead, without him seeing, when we were leaving the house, I put two pairs of my mother's underwear on, on top of mine, and managed to bring them that way.

"I'm going to tell you a secret: one morning, instead of going to school, I went to the cemetery. I thought that if the disease that had killed my mother was so terrible, then maybe it would kill me too. But I couldn't find the grave. I walked for three hours between those dirty stones, covered in pigeon poo and the smell of dog and cat pee. I walked past Mrs. Kravetz and Mr. Guilmann, who had died two years ago, and the Borenstein brothers and my best friend Molke Kreiman's grandparents, but I couldn't find the place where they had put my mother, and I couldn't keep searching because Mr. Levín, who was the cemetery caretaker, found me and chased me with a stick until I had to leave, but a few days later we found out that some Nazis had beaten him and smashed almost all the gravestones, and I didn't care because he had treated me very badly, it even made me a little happy to think that they had done that to him and his stupid graves.

"I learned to speak Spanish because we were in Veracruz for six months and my father sent me to school. But I didn't forget German, I will never forget it, and when I grow up and Hitler is burning in hell I will go back to live in Germany. If you like, you can come with me."

"I can't. I will stay here forever, inside my house."

"That isn't true. One day you will leave."

"Ana, is Berlin far?"

"Yes."

"How will you get there if Amsterdam Street will always bring you back here again?"

"You're crazy like my grandfather. Do you want me to go?"

"No."

"Do you like me?"

"I don't know."

"Touch me. Here, on my breasts. They've grown already. They're big, don't you think?"

"Yes."

"I'll let you kiss them."

"I don't want to."

"In Berlin we used to kiss in the bathrooms at school. And touch each other, all over our bodies. Like this, look."

Ana turned off the light in the bedroom and sat next to Galo. First she kissed his lips and then forced his mouth open with her tongue and stuck it in. Meanwhile, she began to masturbate him with her right hand. Galo didn't move. He was sitting on Ana's bed and he let her do what she wanted, until he felt the strong urge to cry. Ana sat back and looked at him seriously.

"If you tell your mother what we did she'll punish you. And the Nazis will come one night and put hot coals underneath your bed so that you burn. They will tie your hands and feet together and the fire will cover your body in blisters and you will shout like you would in hell."

Galo said to her, unable to stop crying, "I don't want that to happen to me."

"Do you want me to hug you?"

"Yes."

Ana hugged Galo, and they stayed like that for a moment until they heard the front door opening. Then she got up and switched on the light and sat back down at the table, and before her father came into the room she was already reading her grade five history textbook.

13

THEY HAD FINISHED eating dinner. Ana and Galo had gone to bed. The man and Galo's mother found themselves alone in the kitchen. They cleared away the plates and the mother made him try the milk curd pudding that she had prepared, and after eating a little they looked at one another for a long while, and the mother locked the door with a key, and without saying a word they began to kiss and lay down on the table. Afterwards, despite his words getting tangled, the man began to speak:

"I was in charge of accounting, and Rebecca spent all day in the perfumery. She was an excellent saleswoman. That's where she met him. One afternoon a group of angry men arrived and started throwing stones at the windows. They wanted to come in and smash the bottles of perfume and cologne, but he stopped them. They became friends and then lovers, and a year later Rebecca came into my office and told me she was leaving me, that she was going to go and live with him. She didn't even say goodbye to Ana or her father. She didn't take any clothes. She just left.

"When Ana got home from school I told her that her mother had fallen ill and that she was in the hospital. I spoke to my father-in-law and we decided that, as far as Ana was concerned, Rebecca was going to die. A month later we told her that her mother had died and that she couldn't go and visit her grave in the cemetery. Six months later the government forced my father-in-law to hand over his factory, and the only surviving traces of my life came crashing down around me.

"One day before we left, I went to see Rebecca. She was very thin. I told her we were leaving and I offered her the chance to change her mind and come with us. She said no, that her new husband was creating false documents for her, so that she could pass as German, and she begged me to leave Ana with her, that she would be happier there than in a strange new country."

He fell silent. He lit a cigarette and turned to face her. Galo's mother's eyes were closed. She could still feel the heat of another body on her skin.

"Do you think I did the right thing?"

"I don't know."

"Tell me something about your life. Tell me something about yourself. Or ask me whatever you want."

"Did Rebecca have blue eyes?"

14

SINCE GALO NEVER LEFT the house, and since his mother, ever since her husband had left her, was always absolutely discreet about her business, it was very unlikely that their Amsterdam Street neighbours would find out what was going on. However, the day arrived when the mother, moved by what she had begun to feel for Ana's father, confessed to the priest. Apart from severely reprimanding her, the priest also told her that the news was already making the rounds in the neighbourhood, and that the neighbours hadn't needed anybody to tell them.

"Are you crazy, Guadalupe? Do you want your soul to go straight to hell? And your son? Even if you care so little about your own life that nothing matters to you anymore, what about Galo? Haven't you thought about him? It's crazy enough that you have rented out those rooms. I didn't say anything because you needed the money, but now you come and tell me you've fallen in love? For God's sake, Guadalupe! I shouldn't even be speaking to you. Everyone is talking about what goes on in your house. Don't you feel even a little bit ashamed of yourself? Your neighbours are watching! Those people are eventually going to take over our community, and then the entire city! They have already built their temples, their schools, they walk around wearing their little hats and their children congregate in the park to sing in foreign languages in the most insolent way, and you act as though none of it mattered . . . I warned you, Guadalupe, ever since your husband went off with that woman I told you: devote yourself to God and find a good man who will have you along with your son. But you didn't listen, you waited and waited and now it's your flesh and not your head that's in charge. You didn't provide for it in time and now it demands you sleep with the first man to come along! What, was there nobody at the market who would do you the favour? Don't you know those people are wicked? Why do you think the government is letting them into the country? Because they wish to destroy us! They don't want there to be a single Catholic left! Not only will they take over this neighbourhood, they will kill us all, they will close down our churches again! Don't you understand? Have you already forgotten the tragedy we went through only a few years ago? How many more martyrs must die in the name of the church before you to open your eyes? This has to end. . . . If you don't kick them out of your house I will be forced to request that the archbishop excommunicate you."

But Galo's mother could not obey the priest. It didn't matter that every second or third night someone would leave a bag of excrement in front of the entranceway, or that once someone painted an enormous red swastika on one of the windows. It didn't matter because, every night, after eating a dinner of herring and bitter cucumber and the cold meats the man would bring from Burakov's shop, she would need to feel the heat of his body and they would wait for the children to go to bed before lying down on the kitchen table.

In any case, the archbishop didn't have to excommunicate her, because the man received a letter by special post informing him that Mount Sinai Beneficence's board of directors had arranged for the migration department to provide the necessary documents to allow him to work as an accountant in the country, and furthermore had gotten the Morning Mist aftershave factory, in the city of Guadalajara, to take him on as their manager.

"Once I'm settled I will send money so that you and Galo can come and live with us in Guadalajara," Ana's father said.

The woman did not believe him. And she was right: they never saw each other again.

Ana and Galo said goodbye up on the roof.

"What's Guadalajara like?"

"I don't know."

"Promise me you will never let another woman kiss you like I did."

"I promise."

"Say: 'I swear on the graves of Moses and Joshua that I will never kiss again.'"

"I swear on the graves of Moses and Joshua that I will never kiss again."

"'If I do not keep this promise then Hitler will come and put hot coals underneath my bed.'"

"If I do not keep this promise then Hitler will come and put hot coals underneath my bed."

"Good. Now I am going to kiss you and it will be the last kiss you ever get."

And Ana kissed him on the mouth for three minutes and then climbed down from the rooftop.

And Galo stayed up there looking towards Ajusco, where the clouds first went red and then grey, and he felt for the first time that his life was nothing.

When he went down the man and Ana and the grandfather were getting into a taxi. He went to sit in his chair and watched the bougainvillea's first flower for a long time. He watched as his mother found the sign that said "two rooms for rent" inside one of the rooms and went to hang it on the door.

He felt calmer after he realized that it did not matter how far away Guadalajara was, because Amsterdam Street would eventually bring Ana back again.

15

THE DAY GALO heard Toño Bermúdez say that two cities had disappeared beneath enormous mushrooms, the patio flooded.

He had to put the chair inside his room and spend the entire morning using a bucket to throw out the water, while he thought about what it would be like to disappear beneath a mushroom. Because Toño Bermúdez did not let anything interrupt his slot on the radio that morning, not even the voice of Carlos Gardel, he couldn't stop talking about what had happened. His voice choked with emotion, he repeated the cables from the news agencies several times and commented that, after what had happened, the world had to ask itself who was humanity's real enemy: the Nazis and their Japanese and Italian allies, or the President of the United States, who was capable of giving the order to drop bombs that disintegrated a human body to such an extent that it could blow away in the wind.

The bougainvillea was to blame for the flood. The storm the night before had ripped off almost all of its leaves, and the water on the ground had turned them into a paste that had blocked the drain.

The mother was furious because somebody was supposed to come to see the rooms that very morning.

After Ana and what was left of her family left for Guadalajara, the rooms were left unoccupied for a long time. These were sad months for Galo and his mother, because she had not yet forgotten about the heat of the man's body on top of the kitchen table, and neither had Galo forgotten about his last kiss with Ana on the rooftop nor the fact that it would be his last.

Once he managed to unblock the drain, the water quickly flowed towards the tube hidden beneath the patio floor. It dragged the remaining leaves along with it, the swirling liquid creating a sound Galo had never heard before, or at least had never noticed: it sounded as though the earth was desperately devouring food that it needed, but that it was eating with a disregard or at least indifference to the effort the plant had made to grow it.

That day he also made a very important discovery: the bougainvillea would not die from the enormous loss it had sustained. It was able to endure the falling of its flowers like he could endure the absence of the people he loved, and this strengthened the fellowship that Galo felt with the plant, despite the fact that its stems were growing quickly, wrapping themselves around the nails in the wall, reaching about halfway, while he was still less than a metre and a half tall.

16

THE NEW TENANT was a hairdresser who had arrived in Mexico from Spain seven years earlier.

The first thing Galo's mother did was ask the priest if this man belonged to a wicked people too. The priest told her she could rent him the rooms, but that she should be careful, because the only Spaniards coming to Mexico lately were the Reds, and being a Red could be just as dangerous as being a Jew.

He was a fat man, with very little hair on his head. He didn't have a moustache, but, as Galo soon found out, he knew more about moustaches than anybody else. "If you don't turn out to be hairless like most of your race, one day it will grow and you will realize that a moustache must be looked after, trimmed, brushed. A moustache, young man, is like your bougainvillea: If you want it to grow strong and healthy, you must care for it every single day," he told the boy. Since a soft fuzz was beginning to grow on Galo's upper lip he listened attentively, although he still hadn't decided whether or not he would grow a moustache when he grew up.

In order for the new tenant to turn one of the rooms into the hairdressing salon he needed, he had to engage in battle with Galo's mother. Some important modifications were needed, such as knocking down the wall that faced the street in the largest bedroom to build a door and a very large window, not to mention positioning the revolving cylinder with spirals of colour next to the new door, and putting a sign above it saying "Guernica Hairdresser" and underneath, in smaller lettering, "Supervised by Mr. Clodomiro Santibáñez, official ex-hairdresser of the fourth infantry brigade of the government of the Spanish Republic." And the worst of it was that in the middle of the room a swivelling chair had to be installed, and for this four holes had to be drilled into the floor, to make sure it was fixed in place, so that those who sat in it "would feel comfortable and, most importantly, stable, because when somebody sits here they should feel the same security and trust they feel when they sit down on the toilet to shit," Mr. Santibáñez explained to them.

Galo felt excited about the salon, and when the hairdresser found out that he didn't go to school and that he was destined to be nobody because he couldn't become a carpenter, Mr. Santibáñez asked the mother if she would allow him to hire her son as an assistant and apprentice, and from that moment onwards, along with carrying out the chores he had at home, he became the assistant and apprentice to the hairdresser.

He would have to sweep the floor to collect the hundreds of thousands of bits of hair that fell as the scissors went to work; wash the combs; fill up the water, cologne, and talc receptacles; oil the clipper so that the small spring would move the blade without any snags; keep the razor sharp; arrange the chairs where the clients would sit and wait their turn; tidy up the magazines and newspapers; and fill up the bowl of candy, so that the last thing the person who had sat in the chair would receive, before walking out onto the street to show off their haircut, was a touch of sweetness.

"One should leave this place with the nape of their neck feeling fresh, their hair smelling of cologne, and a sweet taste in their mouth," Mr. Clodomiro Santibáñez explained to Galo, "that will be one of the most effective means at our disposal to promote this hairdresser."

═══

However, despite having completed the renovations that transformed their biggest room into a salon — which looked very elegant from the street — and despite having a very enthusiastic assistant, it was not easy for Clodomiro Santibáñez to get the neighbours to warm to him, because only three blocks away on Amsterdam Street was Eternal Madrid, supervised by the hairdresser José Francisco Vicente, who although he was also Spanish, was not the kind who had just arrived, but the kind who had been living in the city for hundreds of years. But Mr. Santibáñez had one advantage: he had fought in the war, and in war, he explained to Galo, one learns many things about tactics and strategy. In order to convince them to abandon Eternal Madrid and choose Guernica, he employed two secret weapons.

The first was twofold: the purchase of a shortwave radio that he tuned to the English and French news bulletins that were broadcast for America, and the presentation of himself as an authorized distributor of *Die Shtime* (which was written in Yiddish) and the *Voz Republicana*. It was as if he had planted sweet-smelling flowers in a forest because, as soon as word spread, the hairdresser's shop became filled with Jews and Spanish anarchists and communists who buzzed around like excited bees. He took these actions because, before defining his combat strategy, Clodomiro Santibáñez studied the situation in great detail and realized that most of these people who had come to live in the area surrounding Amsterdam Street were Europeans like himself, some of them Jewish and others Red Spaniards, just as the priest had warned Galo's mother, while others were Mexicans, but artists and intellectuals who were just as worried about what was happening in Europe as the Europeans themselves.

The second secret weapon was aimed at the young. They didn't seem to have any interest at all in listening to the radio or reading the newspapers. They didn't care that in Nuremberg a court was set up to try the Nazi leaders, nor that the atomic explosions in Hiroshima and Nagasaki would have unforeseeable consequences, nor about the horrors of the concentration camps and that even that the most optimistic of estimates talked about sixty million deaths, nor how the Spanish in Spain were able to endure Franco who had rather mysteriously managed to hold on to every last bit of power; they didn't care because deep down and despite some of them eating marinated herring and kosher meat and others eating butifarra and chorizo, and despite the fact that, up until a few years ago, they had gone to sleep listening to Catalan, Basque, and Yiddish lullabies, they had now tried tamales, tacos, and enchiladas, and they were beginning to think that they would not be like their fathers or their uncles or their older brothers, and that sooner or later they would forget everything they needed to forget and they would turn into authentic Mexicans.

For them he placed ten pornographic magazines under the pile of *Die Shtime* and *Voz Republicana*.

The strategy worked. The men went so that their beards would be trimmed and their moustaches looked after while they read and listened to the BBC from London or the French stations, and the young people would sit and wait on the chairs as they flicked sneakily through the magazines. In less than two months, Guernica Hairdresser was full every afternoon.

=====

Santibáñez introduced himself to everyone by saying that his fame as a hairdresser did not only originate from his work in Madrid and Barcelona, and on other battlefields, but also because as soon as he arrived in Mexico, General Cárdenas had taken him on as his personal hairdresser, and that it was he, Santibáñez, who had tended to his hair and moustache during his final years as president.

"Three hours before General Cárdenas went out onto the balcony of the National Palace to tell the world that he had decided to expropriate the oil companies, I, Clodomiro Santibáñez, and let me be struck by a bolt of lightning right at this moment if I am not telling you the truth, trimmed his moustache. Imagine how nervous the general must have felt in that moment. However, in the midst of the chaos and the agitation of his ministers and secretaries, he asked all of them to leave his office for a moment and demanded my presence. When I entered, he was already sitting in his favourite chair. He greeted me with a smile, like he did every time we saw one another, as if this was no different from any other day, and he said what he always said: 'Clodomiro, do what you do best.' But that time he added: 'I want my moustache to look better today than it ever has,' and he closed his eyes and relaxed so that my scissors could work freely and with concentration, because he knew that, more than his demeanour, or how shiny his shoes were or how well-ironed his jacket, the most important thing at that moment was that his moustache be perfect."

Galo heard many times that the clients did not believe the stories about Cárdenas, but nobody dared contradict Clodomiro directly because, liar or not, he always left their hair and moustaches looking excellent and they didn't want to run the risk of being expelled from that small paradise that had been born on Amsterdam Street, where they could read their newspapers and listen to the news, and argue over and over again — in the case of the Spanish, about whether or not a National Front under the leadership of the Communist Party or an armed movement could oust Franco, and in the case of the Jews, if they should assimilate in Mexico or continue to think about the constitution of the national Jewish state in the distant desert lands of Palestine.

"You know what, Galo, I have a dream that recurs so often that I think one day it will come true. One day Franco, the son-of-a-thousand-bitches, comes in and sits in this very chair and asks me to tidy up his moustache. So I put a little foam on him and start to trim the ends, and when he thinks I am just about to finish, I begin to shout, my mouth right next to his ear, the names of all the comrades shot by his damn Civil Guard, one by one, and I shave his moustache off completely, leaving his upper lip absolutely bare.

"I always wake up after Franco looks in the mirror, his eyes wide, and realizes that without his moustache he cannot possibly continue to govern Spain."

17

D URING HIS FIRST WEEKS as the assistant and apprentice to the hairdresser, Galo would gather the hair and the moustache trimmings that fell onto the floor into a bag, and on Tuesdays and Saturdays, which were the days when the garbage trucks made their rounds, he would leave it on the street, and on the days when they did not come he would burn the bag on the patio of the house.

It was sometime later that he realized he didn't have the right. Those coils of hair, all different shades and lengths, had witnessed what had happened to Mr. Santibáñez's clients, so throwing them away or burning them was like throwing away or burning bodies that, before arriving in Mexico, had come very close to being burned or thrown away in Europe. He also felt it would be terrible to mix different hair together, as though they were useless leftovers, as if the light brown hair that had belonged to Santiago Ordorica, who had escaped being shot on the outskirts of Girona and crossed the border into France on foot and who had spent six months in a concentration camp before finally boarding a boat that took him to a new continent, were the same as the curly grey hair that belonged to Jacob Lindberg, the first violin in the Vilna symphony orchestra, whose father and sister Molka, naked and hungry, had run to hide in the woods where the dogs trained by the German army had forced them to climb a tree from which the soldiers later hanged them.

Galo felt he didn't have the right to mix the hairs, because if they had been saved from all of that, it was unfair that they should end up in a bonfire or mixed in with thousands of tonnes of bottles and chicken heads and pig entrails and biscuit boxes in the city's garbage dump.

"If I allow these hairs to disappear," Galo thought, "what will happen when Mr. Lindberg or Mr. Ordorica die? Where will something of them, their memory, be left? How will we know how difficult it was for Ordorica to cross the mountains that lay between Spain and France on foot, or what Lindberg felt when he saw the bodies of his father and his sister swaying beneath the branches of a tree in the Vilna forest?"

And so he began to sweep the floor immediately after any client he decided he must rescue from the flames or the trash. So, while Santibáñez's precise scissors began to work on the next client, and a few of the young men began to flip through the pornographic magazines, and the shortwave radio was announcing something about a street in Berlin that would cease to be a street because it would be cut in two by a cement wall and barbed wire, Galo would wrap up the fallen hair in newspaper and later take it up to the roof and put it underneath the water tank so that it wouldn't get wet.

In order to identify them, he started to mark each package with a different colour. José Morlans was green, Rabbi Benjamín Cann was yellow, the poet Antonio Garfias was black, and he went on like this, one by one, until he ran out of colours, and he began to put two stripes of colour on each bundle: one blue line and one brown line was the painter Zizek, who had been beaten by his neighbours when they discovered he had been hiding a Jew in his house; the green line with the black line was a man whose testicles had been crushed to force him to confess who was in charge of the anarchist press in Santiago de Compostela; the yellow and red was for a puppeteer who watched a guard blind his mother by burning her pupils with matches in Treblinka . . . and for many months, in the moments when he didn't have anything to do, Galo would go up to the roof and sit facing the hundreds of little packages and try to get straight in his head who each one of those men had been, and, thanks to that, Galo, who couldn't become a carpenter and who had decided not to leave his house because Amsterdam Street would always bring him back again, was introduced to many places in Europe, and he learned a thing or two about the human soul.

One package took him to a small village in Bessarabia, where a man gathered potatoes and onions every morning, and at night when the winds blew he would meet his family to pray in a synagogue; another to a hot and light-filled Saturday at six in the afternoon on a street in Barcelona, where a boy tried to get his football down from a roof while his father was struck in the heart by the first of thousands of bullets fired by the Falange to finish off the resistance and with it the Republican dream; and another package took him to a bench in a square in Hamburg where a young man declared his love to a woman. Because Mr. Santibáñez's clients, although it was true that they were almost always arguing and fighting or searching for different ways of fixing the world in voices that were deep and hoarse and hurried, arrived some days with eyes obscured by a fog of tenderness that Galo learned to recognize as they walked through the door. And on those very special days the clients would relax and in a calm and soft voice recount their memories in such a detailed manner that those who were listening could smell the storm or feel the heat of the sun or the breeze the storyteller had felt back then. And on those days, as though they had come to an agreement without having to say anything, everyone would go quiet. It seemed to Galo that they used those moments to soar over the ocean and arrive at places where they had loved and laughed and fought and prayed, in the place where their hair and their fingers and their legs and their hearts had experienced a sunset for the first time, and where they had felt excited about a colour or a smell or a flavour, and then the monotonous and harsh sound of Mr. Santibáñez's scissors would bring them back to the present moment, there, in Guernica Hairdresser, in a house on Amsterdam Street, where Galo, without their noticing, would gather up their moustache trimmings so that they wouldn't be lost, so that the bodies that had been burned and thrown away, a fate which the clients had escaped, would not be forgotten.

On the roof, gazing at the hundreds of small packages of hair wrapped in newspaper, Galo learned a thing or two about the human soul and also remembered Ana's last kiss, Mr. Gueiser's bottle of perfume, and between thoughts about the world's large and small problems, he remembered his father, how his saw rose and fell as monotonous and harsh as Mr. Santibáñez's scissors, filling the patio with the smell of resin and sawdust, and who had had to leave the country because the president had decided to snatch the oil from the hands of the foreign companies.

18

"THERE YOU HAVE IT. That's why you think the way you do. You people have been living here longer than we have, and what have you done? You sold them a few metres of cheap cloth, you built three or four churches with no crosses or saints, and nothing more. We, on the other hand, have been changing the face of this country ever since we arrived," the poet Antonio Garfias said to Rabbi Benjamín Cann one afternoon when they had both turned up drunk at the hairdresser.

"What an unbelievably stupid thing to say, Antonio, in part because you people aren't doing anything that the Mexicans couldn't do themselves without you. And even if they couldn't, it would be for the best. What good can a bunch of intellectuals do for a country of starving Indians?"

"The general always used to tell me that our arrival would do Mexico a lot of good," Santibáñez interjected, as he measured Morlans the Catalan's left sideburn with a goldsmith's precision.

"If Cárdenas ever said that, it was because he couldn't think of anything else to say. He had already brought you here, and it's not easy to admit having made a mistake when you are that important. Besides he was thinking about the country that was in his mind, not the one beneath his feet."

"That is absurd," howled Garfias, "I have never heard so much nonsense in my entire life!"

"All right," said Cann, as he pinched a corner of his scarf between his fingers to clean the lenses of his glasses, "let's clear something up once and for all, and I hope nobody gets offended. I am going to tell you a story that my grandfather used to tell us. Back before the world was turned upside down, four Jewish Torah scholars had an argument about what would happen if, by the hand of the thousand-times blessed Himself, a man could enter heaven and then leave again.

"'He would die the moment he returned to earth,' said one.

"'He would run to the mountains and stay there, as far away from us as possible,' said another.

"'He would ask for permission to live inside the synagogue for the rest of his life,' said another.

"Efraín Yankelevich, the eldest of the four, said to them:

"'If by the power of the Eternal and thousand-times blessed, a man could get into heaven and then leave again, he would return to earth shrouded in the most absolute saintliness, and with every step he took in his days left alive, he would provide us with love and kindness and certainty. He would never be unjust again.'"

Cann stopped talking and silence descended. Nobody present appeared to understand the meaning of the story.

"I don't see what this story about your grandfather has to do with what we are talking about," said Garfias.

"Think about it backwards," the rabbi said to him, still rubbing his glasses with his scarf. "Turn the best place in the world into the worst, heaven into hell, and you will know what I am trying to say."

"You aren't trying to say anything at all . . . damn it just go ahead and tell us what you want to say!" Garfias shouted, now clearly exasperated.

"If the man is made holy upon entering heaven, what happens to he who steps one foot into hell, even if it was only once? Nothing good can come from someone who has been there. What did your people and mine bring here in our suitcases? Shit! Resentment, panic, nightmares, disappointment! Can you compare any of these things with any deed, as good as it may seem? Behind our synagogues and our stores and our chants and behind your research institutes and your philosophers and poets and economists, you can just make out a thousand faces of horror . . . don't you understand? With every step we take, your people and mine, like any refugee who has come here escaping fascism, sow the seeds of poison and putrefaction . . . don't you realize? Look! We spend hours and hours trying to prove who has suffered the most, been beaten the most, endured the worst destruction, and then we immediately argue about who can offer the most to Mexico! And another thing," said Rabbi Cann, his voice trembling, "I'm sick of hearing you all say that even if Franco were to fall you wouldn't leave this place. And Jews say it too; we are always saying that, even if the Germans got down on their knees and begged us to come back . . . and we all repeat it again and again because we claim we have fallen in love with this land, but it isn't true. If we want to stay here it's because over there we would go right back to being the sons of any ordinary neighbour, while here we live like kings thanks to our white skin and our green or blue eyes. We are powerful amongst the Indians, while amongst Europeans we are miserable in lands of misery. Just open your eyes, Antonio, we will never actually love this place! Over and over again when our eyes see a tree grow in Parque México, in our hearts we see the image of the tree we watched grow in our childhoods, and the smell of the rain is never quite right because we instantly close our eyes to remember the way it smelled in our devastated towns and villages, to which we will never be able to return, not only because they will be forever different, but because we will be too!"

"Are you finished?" Garfias asked.

"Yes," replied the rabbi, trying to compose himself.

"Well fuck your philosophy. It wasn't just shit we brought here on our boats, we still have plenty we want to achieve in this world! What you're saying is that the only thing left for us to do is to commit suicide," he said, taking his hat and walking out of the hairdresser and slamming the door.

Cann said nothing. He seemed lost in his own thoughts for a moment until his breathing went back to its normal rhythm. Afterwards, he put his glasses back on and left without saying goodbye. Galo hurried to sweep up a little of Morlans' soul, who was already looking in the mirror to see how his haircut had turned out.

"What neither of them realizes is that it doesn't matter, none of it matters," he said, and then he paid and left.

19

For a few weeks the air around Amsterdam Street was charged with tension. The news of the exchange between the rabbi and the poet had spread to every corner, store, and house. With the thousands of words uttered for or against, Jews and Spaniards built a wall that divided them, and although there were some Jews who did not agree with the rabbi's pessimistic theory, and some Spaniards who did not agree with the poet's optimistic one, they still ended up closing ranks against each other to such a degree that when a Spaniard was inside the hairdresser no Jew would enter, and vice versa. Nobody commented anymore on the news on the radio or argued about the articles that appeared in the newspapers. Santibáñez cut hair in silence, and Galo did not sweep up anybody's memories. The situation was so dire that the young men couldn't even muster the enthusiasm to look at the pornographic magazines.

Santibáñez began to worry, but fortunately neither Cann nor Garfias wished to definitively break off their friendship. One morning when the shop was filled with Jews on account of the approaching Rosh Hashanah, for which they all wanted to tidy up their beards, moustaches, and hair, Garfias came in, clearly remorseful, and faced Benjamin Cann in front of everyone. He said he felt very ashamed of having insulted him so terribly, and as a symbol of their friendship he offered him two bottles of an excellent Rioja that his nephews had sent him and a tin of olive oil from Jaén that he treasured.

The rabbi received these gifts, the expectant gaze of all in the room upon him, and then apologized to Garfias. "If you had to react so explosively, it's only because of what I said, and for this I am sorry," he said. Garfias stretched out his arms and they embraced one another, and, thanks to this embrace, everything went back to normal. As if they had been waiting outside, two Basques and a Galician came in from the street and joined the reconciliation festivities. Santibáñez was so happy that for the first time he twisted the dial of the radio away from the station that broadcast the European news bulletins, and happened to tune in to the program on which Carlos Gardel sang every day, who, as though he had foreseen the success of that morning in the Guernica Hairdresser, sang for them: "Distant Buenos Aires / how lovely you must be now / It's been almost ten years / since you saw me set sail. / I feel as though the memory / stabs its blade into my flesh," and Garfias, delighted to be listening to his favourite tango, stretched out his right hand towards Cann, who took it and danced with him next to the swivelling chair, and Galo, who was listening again to the voice that his father had so loved to hear, Galo, who embraced everyone as if he too had decided to forget for a moment the rabbi's terrible ideas because the important thing now was to dance and sing, told himself that he would have to gather every single strand of hair that would be left on the floor that day.

20

THE MOMENT HE SAW the man, Mr. Rosemberg went pale and his bottom lip began to tremble.

"There isn't enough room in a hairdresser for both a Jew and a German."

Everyone turned to look at the man who had just entered.

Santibáñez, for whom the row between Garfias and Cann just a few days earlier still felt very fresh, had no intention of allowing anyone to dampen the high spirits they had salvaged. He moved towards him.

"This is just what I needed . . . Look, sir, I don't know who you are, but my clients are all Jews or Red Spaniards. Just a few blocks away there's another hairdresser where I am sure you would be welcome."

The German looked at Santibáñez and then turned to look at Mr. Rosemberg. Every pair of eyes was on the German.

"Please, all I want is a haircut."

Santibañéz looked towards Cann and Garfias, whose game of chess had been interrupted, in order to gauge their opinion before answering. They both shrugged slightly to demonstrate their consent.

"All right then," said the hairdresser.

Somebody offered the German their seat, and as soon as he sat down he began to cry. He covered his face with both his hands and wept for ten minutes. Nobody moved. As soon as he calmed down, he began to speak without lifting his gaze.

"I killed him. I killed him with one bullet in his head. I took his pistol from its holster, and I pulled the trigger. When my wife found out that our two children were dead, she slit her wrists and bled to death. That's when I made up my mind. I put on my gala uniform, polished my medals, and walked to the bunker. The end was imminent, and I couldn't let anyone else be the one to do it. It was easy to get in. The few officials left were burning documents, fighting amongst themselves. There were no guards left: they had all run away.

"He was alone, drinking. His shirt was undone down to his belly button, and his suspenders were hanging down next to his legs. In front of him was a lit fireplace. There were a few plates with traces of food and empty champagne bottles on the table. From the radio came the voice of a man shouting orders in Russian. His wife was on the floor, dead.

"He didn't see me. After a while he got up and started to piss into the fire. When he realized what was going on, when he sensed he was about to die, the Führer lowered his head, and as he stared into the flames, said, 'It's better to piss here. The toilet smells like shit.' Then I shot him in the head."

The German stopped talking and a silence fell.

Morlans shattered it.

"'Smells like shit . . .' Those can't have been Hitler's last words."

"Don't listen to him, this man is crazy," said Santibañéz.

"Besides, Hitler isn't dead, he's frozen. Everyone knows he's being kept in a basement in Asuncion," said Garfias.

"What complete nonsense," said Cann.

"I once heard that Gardel was frozen too," said Rosemberg.

"Can you imagine Hitler pissing?" asked Morlans.

"If I knew I would have to listen to this kind of drivel, I would have stayed at home," said Santibáñez.

"We should hang a sign outside that says 'No Aryans allowed.' What do you think, Clodomiro?" said Garfias.

"No, I don't think so," said Santibáñez.

"Why do people feel the need to make things up? As a matter of fact, although it may be a slightly different situation, they made up all that stuff about Jesus going to heaven because nobody knew where his body was, too," said Rosemberg.

"That's because back then nobody was frozen," said Cann.

They kept arguing for a long time, until someone noticed that the German was gone. Then the rabbi decided to open both bottles of Rioja that Garfias had given to him when they had reconciled and that he had left at the hairdresser so that everyone could admire them like trophies, and invited everyone to have a drink, to the health of their families, the death of Hitler, and to Rosh Hashanah, which they had just celebrated.

21

THE HAIRDRESSER WOULDN'T let Galo look at the pornographic magazines for fear of getting into trouble with his mother, who, thanks to the advice of the priest, was now always on the lookout for possible transgressions.

Since she had let Santibañéz convert her rooms into Guernica Hairdresser, the mother had had constant trouble with the priest and a few neighbours, not because they had anything against hairdressers, but because foreigners gathered there as if it were a social club and so their Mexican neighbours felt out of place. "We Mexicans have to show our passports to get into your house," they would say to her at the market. She didn't pay them any attention, because Santibáñez paid her double what she had asked for, and because her son seemed busy and content.

But Galo began to feel very curious about the magazines. As he swept the floor to collect the cloak of stories left behind after every job, he had noticed how a few boys who looked at them would touch themselves inside their trousers, with their right hands in their pockets, and would get very nervous, and while Santibáñez was busy preparing soap foam with his back to them, they would move their hand faster inside their trousers. One afternoon when the hairdresser was closed, because it was Sunday, Galo went inside, looked at the magazines carefully, and started to touch himself too. That night he dreamed that Ana was kissing him.

That was one day before the Guernica Hairdresser had its moment of glory and definitively entered the history books, and Clodomiro Santibáñez became a figure loved and respected by all, because just after five in the afternoon none other than Lázaro Cárdenas himself walked in.

22

====

WHEN THE DOOR OPENED and the outline of the general's body appeared in its frame, Benjamin Cann and Antonio Garfias were waiting for their turn in the swivelling chair, and the hairdresser was adding the final touches to Pedro Valle's hair. Galo was helping by holding up a mirror behind the client's head.

"Good afternoon, Clodomiro," said Cárdenas.

Pedro was the first one to see him in the mirror, but he said nothing because astonishment made the air catch in his throat.

Cann and Garfias turned to face the door and immediately got to their feet. Cann took off his black hat and Garfias buttoned up the shirt he had undone when the conversation had begun to suffocate him. Cárdenas smiled at the two men and walked up to Santibáñez, his hand outstretched.

"Since you never came to see me, I had to come here instead. Would you be able to cut my hair and tidy up my moustache?"

"Of course, my General," said Santibáñez, knowing that in that moment his reputation had reached incalculable heights.

Pedro Valle got up from the chair as if he had been catapulted upwards. Cárdenas went to sit down but first he turned to look at the two waiting men.

"Forgive me gentlemen, would you mind letting me go before you? I'm in a bit of a hurry."

Since neither of them said anything, Cárdenas settled down in the chair, stretched out his legs and closed his eyes.

"Go ahead, Clodomiro, do what you do best."

Santibáñez silently placed the cleanest apron in the drawer across the general's chest, fixed it around the back of his neck, and got to work, a large smile fixed on his face.

Cann and Garfias said their goodbyes in a hurry, saying they would come back in a little while.

"Why did you disappear?" said Cárdenas. "You have no idea how many people I had to ask in order to track you down."

"I'm sorry, General, I thought you had returned to Michoacán after you left office."

"I come and go. And you, what have you been up to?"

"Working, as you can see."

While Santibáñez manoeuvred his scissors and chatted with his friend, and a few curious people gathered on the street outside because Pedro had been running around shouting to anyone who would listen that Lázaro Cárdenas was in the hairdresser's shop, Galo did not take his eyes off the man who was now chatting in a relaxed manner and allowing his hair to be styled as if he wasn't guilty of anything, as if he had nothing to do with his father leaving with the woman with blue eyes, the one whose arm his mother had sawn off, as if he didn't know that he had changed Galo's destiny forever, just when Galo had had to accept he would be nothing because he couldn't be a carpenter. Galo remembered that had it not been for this act, his mother would not have said that her son would never leave the house, and as he remembered all of these things that had happened to him, he plucked up the courage to interrupt the conversation between the two friends, and almost without knowing what words were coming out of his mouth, Galo asked Santibáñez if he would be allowed to trim the general's moustache.

"Please, sir, let me do it," Galo said to Santibáñez, and the hairdresser looked at him as though he were a madman talking nonsense, but he didn't get the chance to give him an answer because it was the general who spoke, who opened his eyes and looked at Galo and smiled and asked, "Who are you?" and Galo replied that he had been Mr. Santibáñez's assistant and apprentice for almost a year now, and then Cárdenas, who valued children very much, told the hairdresser he was so fond of, whom he had tracked down for several years, to let the apprentice take his first steps as a hairdresser by trimming his very own moustache, and, since he was so audacious, that he might as well shave his chin too.

And so Galo dragged over one of the waiting chairs and placed it next to the swivelling chair, clambered onto it and started to work on the face of General Lázaro Cárdenas, the ex-president of Mexico, expropriator of oil, and a saint, according to the rural workers of Michoacán, the workers' syndicates, and the Spanish who hated Francisco Franco with every fibre of their being.

Without climbing down from the chair and under the curious and distrustful eye of Santibáñez, Galo prepared a bottle of soap foam and sharpened the blade against the strip of leather that hung from the chair.

But he had to stop working because, just when he had finished covering Cárdenas' face with the foam, the rabbi and the poet came back, this time accompanied by around twenty Jews and Spaniards who had brought gifts for the general.

Those who had arrived with the rabbi had first rushed to Mr. Burakov's butcher shop and had brought him tins of herring and sour pickles, and those who had come with Garfias had first stopped at the Barbasano family's corner store and had brought him a litre of olive oil, three kilos of sausage, and black pudding with onion.

The Spanish would never forget all the help they had received from Cárdenas when setting themselves up in Mexico. The Jews loved him too, despite the fact that, before declaring war on the man who had died urinating on the flames of a fire, he had threatened to send oil for the thirsty Nazi ships and submarines if the United States and England continued to bear a grudge over Cárdenas taking over their oil companies.

Cárdenas, who was a timid and subdued man despite being a former general and president, received the gifts with great gratitude and warmth, and he had no choice but to listen to the speeches made up on the spot by Garfias and Cann, despite not having had the time to wipe the foam off his face or remove his apron due to the surprise of the gathering and the speed at which the crowd had invaded the place.

With tears in his eyes, Garfias reminisced about the 13th of June, 1939, the day he arrived at the port of Veracruz, and how he and everyone who travelled with him on the *Sinaia* longed to meet their great benefactor, and he promised the ex-president that they would always be his faithful followers.

Cann told Cárdenas that he wished to invite him to see the new synagogue they were building, and that it just so happened that there was a girl here with him, who, by way of thanking him for everything he had done for the Jewish community, was going to sing him a song, and the girl emerged from among the legs of all the men who had filled the hairdresser, with a huge pink bow on top of her head. Rabbi Cann lifted her up onto the chair which Galo had put there in order to shave the general, and that Galo now had to vacate, and from there, her hands clasped behind her back, the girl sang the hymn of the Warsaw Ghetto Uprising in Yiddish, which began with the words: "Never say that you have reached the very end . . ." but just when the general thought that the show was over, Garfias and his people, not about to be outdone, sang the hymn of the rural workers from the Comarca Lagunera: "Brave peasant, plant an idea / that lights up the space like a torch / Make the nation great for your own good / with no other god except Socialism in your soul."

At the end everybody applauded, and Cárdenas had to stand to have his photo taken with the group of Spaniards and Jews, who began to leave one by one with a series of handshakes, first with the general and then with Clodomiro Santibáñez, who from that day onwards they would admire not just for his skills in the art of hairdressing, but also because everything he had told them about his friendship with Cárdenas was true.

———

The general would never forget that afternoon, but not because of the memory of the small crowd that had showered him with praise, songs, and cold cuts, but because of what would happen just a few moments later. When he finally returned to the swivelling chair, Galo, who had been watching and listening to everything from a corner of the room, went back to work. Cárdenas slowly began to relax again, and when Galo saw he was on the verge of falling asleep, he shouted into the general's ear that taking the oil companies away from the men from the United States and England hadn't gone at all well for him, and that it was his fault that his father had to leave the country forever without having first shown him how to be a carpenter. And while he said all this, while Santibáñez watched him, astonished, Galo grabbed the blade he had just sharpened, and cut off, in one single and accurate movement, the general's entire moustache.

23

It took five weeks for General Cárdenas' moustache to grow back. He refused to appear in public until then, forcing his personal secretary to cancel three meetings with European diplomats, seven dinners with the president, and an official tour of the north of the country.

It took Clodomiro Santibáñez much less time (only two weeks) to terminate the rental contract. He never spoke of it openly and never forgave Galo for what he had done, and although he admitted to having given the boy the idea by telling him about his dream involving Franco, that very afternoon he began to look for a new place for Guernica. Since plenty of time had passed and the disputes between the old Spaniards and the new had been gradually evaporating, he negotiated with the owner of Eternal Madrid, who owned the establishment, and they joined forces and set up the United Spain Hairdresser.

Galo returned to his chair, and however many times the mother asked him what had happened that terrible afternoon, he never uttered a word.

═══

Galo never regretted what he had done. That day he decided he would never grow a moustache, and that he would once again start to listen to Toño Bermúdez and Carlos Gardel in the patio of the house, while making sure that the bougainvillea kept growing.

24

M ANY THINGS HAD HAPPENED to him since that morning
when, following the sound of the roaring lion, he had
gotten out of bed to sit for the first time in the chair
his father had made for him.

Meanwhile, the bougainvillea had grown to over two metres
tall, becoming an abundant plant that covered almost the entire
wall, which it had spread across thanks to the nails and strings
that Galo had placed there for it year after year.

"The bougainvillea," he said to himself, "has a path to grow
along; she knows, thanks to this path, what direction her life must
take. She lives in order to reach the next nail and the next string.
But I have nothing of the sort. That is no good. I am nothing,
but still I need to know what to live for. To find out, I must think."

And since what he wanted to discover was his life's path,
he decided to think about the only path he knew: Amsterdam
Street. And because, for Galo, to think was first and foremost to
observe, he positioned his chair in such a way that, without putting too much distance between himself and the bougainvillea,
he could see the street when the door was left open. The only
things that stopped him from observing were when the mother
forced him to do a task or if he had to eat, sleep, or go to the toilet.

===

"How many people are trapped like me on Amsterdam Street? There must be so many out there walking around and around, passing the door to my house again and again for eternity."

Occasionally he would try to memorize a person's face, or an item of their clothing, and he waited to see them appear again from the same direction as before, because he thought that might be a good way of measuring time; much better than measuring it in months and days and hours. But sometimes he would lose track of time and of what he was supposed to be thinking about because the desire to see his father, or Ana, would overcome him again.

He realized that very few people came past a second time, and so he thought that time must not be particularly precise when it came to the lives of humans. They could be watching from a street corner as a couple kissed, or reading the headlines of a newspaper that had been left on the table of a café, or looking out of the corner of their eye at a mother feeding her small child, or finding another place to open a hairdresser on the same street, as Clodomiro Santibáñez had done; they might not come past again for a long time, or perhaps never. It's also possible, he thought, that they do come past again, but when they do Galo was distracted, or that he saw but didn't recognize them, perhaps because they no longer looked the way they had the first time he'd seen them. There is also a chance, and this idea worried him a great deal, that not only did people change, but the house did too. What if one of these two things happened to his father: What if he changed so much that Galo didn't recognize him when he walked past, and what if the house was now so different that his father didn't recognize it? What if the only thing he had been doing all these years, since he'd stood before his son, after telling the mother that he would never see her again, was to go round and round in circles along the street without finding the house?

It was the first time Galo had thought about his father in this way. He imagined him walking, exhausted, with a saw in his hand searching for wood to make furniture with, and he thought his father must be dirty, without the daily shower where he would first wash one arm and then the other and then his head and would finish by gargling the water that was inside his mouth. What did he do every morning if he couldn't listen to Toño Bermúdez and then to Gardel? Did he know, for instance, that the war was over?

After thinking this way about his poor father, he remembered Ana. What if she too had walked past this door a few times without recognizing it? And he thought about Ana's grandfather and imagined him walking down Amsterdam Street with his sheet wrapped around his neck, searching for a shower to try to finally bring about his own death, and so, lost in these reflections and others like them, the next days, weeks, and months of Galo's life passed by.

═══

The storms of May came around, and once more he had to get rid of the water that had collected on the patio and unclog the drain because the bougainvillea petals had covered it, and then August's heavy rains arrived, and then the cold and the bluer skies, and then the mother invited her relatives to come and see in the New Year, and between them, they carried the kitchen table out into the patio and ate there, and a very tall and fat cousin, who had returned from the United States a few days earlier, got drunk and in front of everyone shouted that if his aunt would allow it, he could straighten Galo out and make him be like everybody else, that she should let him take Galo to Los Angeles for a while and that would be enough, but she told him to leave her son alone, because it was her fault he was like this. Although she had never told anybody, she still believed that her son was not quite right in the head because he had watched as she'd sawed off the hand of the woman who, despite missing a hand, still managed to steal her husband; but Galo thought she meant something else: that he was like this because she'd told the father that he would never leave the house, and he felt an overwhelming urge to hug his mother.

═══

One morning Galo heard Toño Bermúdez say that it was the hundredth anniversary of the invasion of Mexico by the United States' army, and that it was very important to remember what a certain boy did back then, a boy who, according to Bermúdez, had wrapped himself in a flag and thrown himself off the top of a hill to defend the nation; a hill upon which stood the castle that Galo had seen so many times from the rooftop, the first time being when he had gone up there with Ana, and later when he deposited the packages of hair. It was then that Galo asked himself why so many foreigners came to live in Mexico.

From what he had overheard in the hairdresser's, his impression was that all countries were somewhat similar: all of them had mountains and castles and parks and houses as well as men with moustaches who decided things on behalf of everybody else. So why did they come here? What was so special about Mexico; what did it have that no other country did?

And Galo, who had been sitting in his chair for six months now, observing and thinking, realized that the answer to that question wasn't only going to help him understand the reason why so many foreigners wanted to live in Mexico, but would also finally reveal his life's purpose.

⸻

It was Amsterdam Street, of course.

That street, his street, as he had already begun to realize, was a giant clock. But it was a clock that told the time in a much more exact way than any other, because a clock couldn't measure the urge people had to hang around on a street corner, or in front of a window, or to go into a house and never come out . . . but Amsterdam Street could.

One hour is how long it takes for the long hand to go all the way around a clock. What is the unit of time that measures how long it takes a person to walk past his house, he asked himself, and get back again after going all the way around? Whatever its name may be, Galo told himself, *that* was the true human measurement of time — and the reason for all the problems in the world was the not-knowing of this true human measurement of time. This was why two cities evaporated beneath two enormous mushrooms, and this is why my father had to leave, and this is why Mr. Lindberg had to suffer the misfortune of seeing his sister dangling beneath the branch of a tree in Vilna: because the watches that measure lives do not show the true, human time.

People live their lives believing in clocks that know nothing of true time, and everything goes wrong because they are not measuring the time with the Amsterdam Street clock, and this means that Amsterdam Street is a great treasure, the most important treasure of all, one that could help humanity become better than it has been, and someone should protect it. If for any reason it were to be destroyed, what would happen? The world would be deprived of the knowledge of the true time and would lose the only chance it had of making things better, because if Galo, a person who was nothing because he could not be a carpenter, was thinking all of this, it meant that one day, everybody else, those who were able to become what they had to become, would discover it too and will therefore be able to change everything.

And when will they discover it? He did not know, but whenever it happened Amsterdam Street must be in perfect condition.

Galo's life took an important turn, because from that moment onwards he would no longer be the one who couldn't be a carpenter or the one who never left his house, and neither would he be the one who never learned how to be a hairdresser, because he had found his purpose in life.

Destiny, he thought with growing enthusiasm, had not been arbitrary with him. Things had happened the way they had because he had a very important mission to complete, and now he was able to understand many things, for example why he had turned the roof of his house into a refuge for the souls of the men from the Guernica Hairdresser: because those men's stories needed to be inside the same machinery that measured human time, and this was because the machinery fed on them in order to keep working. This was why he had to take care of the street as if it were humanity's most valued treasure, because not only did it measure time but also (and when this thought came to him, a shiver ran across his whole body, as though he were standing on the edge of an abyss) it was here, on Amsterdam Street, where the time that made the earth go round had been born.

This was why so many foreigners wanted to live in Mexico, and for that very reason somebody needed to once again wrap themselves in a flag, this time not to jump off the Castle of Chapultepec, but to look after this great treasure which for some mysterious purpose was located here, in the place where Galo was born.

Many sensed this, but nobody had yet understood it like he had.

Over the years, destiny had made sure to put the necessary nails and strings into place to lead him to the knowledge that he had been chosen to protect the street.

The afternoon when he finally understood all of this, in the hot month of May 1948, two days after turning fifteen years old, Galo went up to the rooftop and, with the same conviction with which he had promised Ana he would never kiss another woman, and while looking at the packages of hair and moustache trimmings that he had preserved with such care, he solemnly swore that from that moment onwards, he would be the guardian of Amsterdam Street.

25

How would he care for such an important treasure?

What if it was true that Hitler hadn't died, and was actually frozen, and he appeared one day with all of those Germans raising and lowering their arms towards and away from the sky, and they wanted to invade the street? And what if General Cárdenas hadn't just come to Amsterdam Street for a haircut from Santibáñez, but he actually wanted to see with his own eyes how he could plan to expropriate it like he had done with the oil? And what if the potential enemy wasn't as obvious as an army or an ex-president but hid behind the disguise of any ordinary person, and rented the rooms with the secret intention of seizing first the house and then the whole street? Because protecting the bougainvillea was one thing, Galo only had to water it and fix nails and string so it would keep growing, but preventing the victory of an army with cannons and soldiers and planes was another thing altogether.

If the treasure were to fall into their hands, the world would become even worse than it was already: more Mr. Gueisers dragging sheets behind them, more men who would be nothing because they couldn't be carpenters, more cities beneath mushroom-shaped clouds.

He, as the street's guardian, had to be vigilant, to watch over that incredible machine that could save or destroy humanity.

At first he found ways to scare off several tenants he considered suspicious for various reasons, such as Mr. Epigmenio González Avelar, who had come to the city from Torreón, or Mrs. María Mercedes Ontiveros, Blanco's widow, who rented the rooms and set up a grocery store.

But finally he had to confront an enemy against whom he was powerless, when his mother decided to rent the rooms to the priest. Not even scrawling "The church is the scum of the earth" in black paint on the walls of the largest room worked. Clodomiro Santibáñez had told him this phrase once.

The priest needed to use the rooms as classrooms so that the neighbourhood children could take their catechism class while a new classroom was built in the local parish.

Galo realized that the situation was serious, partly because of everything he had heard about the church when he worked in the hairdresser, but above all because, since the very first sessions of the first course, and there were six in total, the priest warned his disciples that they weren't there just to prepare themselves for the sacrament they would make in a few months, but also that, from that moment onwards, they would form a part of God's General Plan to reconquer the world, and to be true soldiers of the Supreme Being they had to fight against the mortal enemies of the Holy Roman Catholic and Apostolic Church, and that these were communists, in the first place, and the Jews were a close second, who had come together in an infernal alliance, and just like they had killed the Saviour, they wouldn't hesitate to kill the Catholics either. "We are here to learn how to fight against the demon and his followers!" the priest would say again and again, and slam his fist against a table. "We will stop them from changing our Christian way of living. We will stop them from conquering the neighbourhood, because if we allow that, then one day they will conquer the city, and then the country, and then the little that remains of the free world. We must be like the Spanish Catholic Falange, who ripped the red cancer out of their country!" And the students learned the lesson quickly, and began to practise how to be soldiers of God's General Plan. On Sunday mornings before going to school, they would cross Parque México and scare the group of young people who had once been friends with Ana, whose skull caps they would pull off their heads and whose side locks they would pull, and they would threaten to burn them in the oven in the bakery that belonged to one of their fathers.

The mother asked Galo to take part in the classes because the priest told her that, despite not being quite right in the head, being confirmed was still an obligation. "Even boys like him have the right to go the Heavenly Kingdom," he assured her. Galo agreed to take the courses since it was the best way of finding out their possible plans of conquest and, when the moment came, making sure he could act swiftly.

As a result of hearing them so often, he learned the Niceno-Constantinopolitan Creed and the Ten Commandments by heart, as well as an old homily for Holy Saturday that the priest was fond of, and despite the fact that the majority of his students would start to yawn or murmur when he recited it, Galo was intensely moved by it.

Today there is a great silence over the earth, a great silence, and stillness, a great silence because the King sleeps; the earth was in terror and was still, because God slept in the flesh and raised up those who were sleeping from the ages. God has died in the flesh, and the underworld has trembled. Truly he goes to seek out our first parent like a lost sheep; he wishes to visit those who sit in darkness and in the shadow of death. He goes to free the prisoner Adam and his fellow prisoner Eve from their pains, he who is God, and Adam's son . . . "I am your God, who for your sake became your son, who for you and your descendants now speak and command with authority those in prison: Come forth, and those in darkness: Have light, and those who sleep: Rise. I command you: Awake, sleeper, I have not made you to be held prisoner in the underworld. Arise from the dead; I am the life of the dead."

When he heard the homily, Galo would close his eyes and almost immediately see the image of his father, wrapped in rags, shivering with cold, the soles of his feet covered in sores, trying in vain to sleep under a shelter after many days of walking around Amsterdam Street again and again, searching for the door of his house. And he saw himself, the son, coming across his father, and stretching out his right hand to stroke the man's head, and letting him curl up against his chest.

In any case, and despite the permanent tension he felt during those years owing to the fear that, right under his nose, a plot was being hatched without him being able to identify it, Galo learned something new about his mission, because if, as the priest told him, everything had gone so terribly since humanity's first moments, if Adam and Eve had betrayed their father's trust, if the Chosen People who later became wicked had betrayed Moses just as he was receiving from their God the rules for living, as if Evil did not exist, and if Jesus Christ had been born to lead mankind down the path to their salvation but had died without anyone having shown much interest, why not believe that Amsterdam Street was something like a fourth opportunity in the Divine Plan for Salvation?

———

When the classroom in the church was finally finished and the priest vacated the rooms, Galo thought he would be able to rest for a while, but only a week later a woman arrived in the early morning saying she wanted to rent them.

He showed her the rooms while he observed her gestures. The woman, dressed rather elegantly, seemed more concerned about knowing who lived in the house than how much the rent was. She agreed to the terms immediately. She paid the first month's rent up front and told him that she and her husband would be living there and that they would have a friend visiting for a few days at the very most. Galo's mother told her what she always told the tenants, that the rooms were rented without furniture, to which the woman replied that it wasn't a problem, they were used to sleeping on the floor if necessary. Galo's mother took the money and left because she was going to be late opening her stall at the market.

"My son will explain everything you need to know," she said. "I'll be back this afternoon."

The haste with which the deal was done made Galo suspicious. Something about the woman was unsettling, although he couldn't say what it was. It didn't make sense to him that a woman who dressed that way could be used to sleeping on a mat on the floor.

The reason for his unease became clear a few hours later when the woman and her husband, a thin man in a suit, lifted several suitcases out of a small truck; one of them fell open as they were carrying them into the rooms, and Galo, who was peeking through one of the windows, saw that it was filled with guns.

26

THE HUSBAND RUSHED to put the guns back inside the suitcase while the woman closed the door and the window, and Galo, frightened, his heart hammering in his chest, went outside to sit down in his chair by the bougainvillea. He needed to think.

The guns seemed to be proof that the couple were what he had been waiting for for nearly eight years. This was confirmation of all his ideas, that he was the guardian of Amsterdam Street, and now the moment had come to show how far he was willing to go to protect it.

His first thought was that he should leave the house and run to Clodomiro Santibáñez in the United Spain Hairdresser and tell him what was happening. He would also tell the poet Garfias and Rabbi Cann, Galo thought, and between the three of them they would certainly be able to organize a large enough army to resist the invasion. Galo did not think that everyone with an interest in Amsterdam Street was bad, in fact he believed the opposite, that many of those Jews and Spaniards he had met at Guernica Hairdresser, pieces of whom he had taken and stored on the roof, and to whom he had listened speak almost always about the terrible state of the world and the need to change it, would give them his support if he asked for it. But first he needed to decide what to say to them. How would he explain everything he knew about humanity's great treasure where the world's true time was born and why it had to be protected with no thought of how dangerous that might be, like the boy who had wrapped himself in a flag to defend the nation? Why would they listen to him?

But the guns were here, in no other place than right in the heart of Amsterdam Street. Had he not predicted that this would happen? Was it not possible that this couple was the advance guard of a powerful army from the United States who that very night would arrive and set up camp in Parque México? Because if that wasn't the case, why had they brought those guns? Or they could be messengers sent by a thawed-out Hitler, or by the ex-president?

His preoccupied speculation was interrupted by the appearance of the woman in the doorway, who then started to walk towards him. She moved calmly, like someone who had packed only shirts and towels in their suitcase.

"My husband and I have to go out for a moment, but a friend of ours is about to arrive," she said, a broad smile on her face. "Would you be a darling and ask him to wait for us?"

The woman went back into her room and then came out with her husband a moment later, who winked at Galo, and then they walked out and onto the street.

Galo didn't understand what was going on. It made no sense at all that the man had winked at him and that the woman could walk around as though she were completely innocent.

Whatever was happening, he couldn't just keep sitting in his chair. He had to take action. He had to go into that room and find out as much as he could.

There was a sleeping mat on the floor in the large room, and they had made a makeshift bed on top of it with a blanket and a pillow. The suitcases were in the small room, arranged one next to the other. Galo opened the first one. It had clothes inside. He opened the second one. It contained books and papers. The third and fourth were filled with guns.

The voice took him by surprise when he was closing the last suitcase.

"What are you doing?"

The man came and stood next to him, and the woman closed the bedroom door behind her. Galo realized that he could no longer keep pretending. His heart was thumping arrhythmically in his chest, and he felt like he was suffocating.

"Get out! I won't let you do anything!" he shouted at the top of his voice, but he didn't have enough air in his lungs and the room began to spin around him at an incredible speed and suddenly everything went dark.

═══

. . . he goes to seek out our first parent like a lost sheep; he wishes to visit those who sit in darkness and in the shadow of death . . .

═══

His bed.

The crucifix above his head.

The night.

He had to sit up in order to listen. He recognized his mother's voice.

"Thank you so much for looking after him. The problem is he hasn't been right in the head ever since he was a little boy. That's why he says things sometimes. But he wouldn't hurt a fly."

"Let me examine him, I'm a doctor."

"He's just sleeping. This has happened before, when I tried to make him leave the house . . . don't worry."

Without actually getting out of bed, he managed to pull himself into a position in which he could see the patio through the open crack of the door. Standing there were the tenant couple, his mother, and another man. He noticed the way the stranger was breathing. He did so with difficulty, as though despite his mouth being open, he wasn't able to fill his lungs with air.

When he saw that the mother was coming towards the room, he lay down and closed his eyes. The mother poked her head inside for a moment and then closed the door completely. She went back to the others.

"He's asleep," she insisted. "I'll see how he's doing tomorrow. Thank you again."

He decided it would be best to remain lying down. He didn't know what he had to do. War, he thought, had been declared.

He waited for a few hours and once he thought his mother was asleep, he got up stealthily and left the room. The lights were on in the rented rooms, and he could hear the quiet murmur of voices inside from the patio. He crept up to one of the windows. The man he didn't know was lying down and breathing as though he had ten meowing cats inside his lungs. The woman and her husband were pacing nervously around the room.

"Damn it, I told you I'm fine!" said the ten-cats man.

"How the hell am I supposed to believe you're fine when you can't breathe?" said the woman's husband.

"It will pass, it always does!"

"Don't be ridiculous, let Rodolfo get your medicine," said the woman.

"Where the hell did I leave it?" asked the stranger, whose breathing was getting worse with every passing minute.

"It doesn't matter, I could find it in any damn pharmacy!" said the husband, his patience wearing thin.

"It's very late, Rodolfo. He's right, it's dangerous now," the woman said.

"The risk of him dying is more dangerous!" the husband shouted at the woman and left the room, heading directly towards the street without looking towards the window. Galo kept listening.

"Well, rest now and when Rodolfo returns . . ."

"I told you both not to worry about me."

"Would a cup of tea help?"

"No, just . . . the inhaler will help . . . This is a damn nightmare!"

"If you don't calm down it could get worse, couldn't it?"

"Yes."

"So you have to try to relax. God damn it, you in the middle of an attack and now this thing with the boy, who knows if we'll be able to stay here . . ."

"Didn't you hear the mother when she said he isn't right in the head?"

"That may the case, but he's still ruined everything. This place seemed perfect, and now we're going to have to leave. We told you, he saw the guns."

"Wait, we do nothing. Let me speak to him tomorrow. Let's see what happens."

Galo heard the door from the street opening and hid in the toilet so that the man returning with a package in his hand wouldn't see him. He sat down on the toilet.

When he heard the door to the large room close, he came out of the toilet and lay down in his bed. He slept a little before the sun came up.

27

"I HAVE TO CATCH FOUR CATS. Could you help me?"

When Galo woke up, his mother was no longer next to him, and the stranger standing in the doorway was looking at him as though he had been waiting for Galo to wake up. Galo sat up.

"What for?" Galo asked him, and then remembered that last night the man standing in front of him was breathing as though he had ten cats meowing inside his lungs.

"I have to take them to a laboratory to do some tests."

Galo tried to look past the man, out to the patio. He felt uneasy.

"Your mother went to work. My friends did too. Shall we go and look for cats?"

He could see the stranger clearly now. He was young and thin. He had a large and square forehead, and his gaze seemed to fix upon whatever he looked at. Galo felt very confused; they were talking about catching cats and not about the war that had been declared. He decided to keep the conversation going to see what the man wanted.

"Maybe," Galo said, "but I don't leave my house."

"Why?"

"I can help you find cats on the roof. Sometimes they gather up there."

As soon as he said it, he realized he had made a terrible mistake: if they went up to the roof the stranger would see the packages. But it was too late. The man, with the agility of a tiger, was already figuring out how to get up there. Galo put on his trousers and shoes and ran after him, shirtless.

Once they were up on the roof, the stranger looked out towards the volcanoes, breathing deeply. Galo watched him while keeping an eye on the packages wrapped in newspaper that were peeking out from under the water tank.

"I climbed the Popo a while ago," he said to Galo. "Have you ever been?"

"No, I already told you I don't leave my house."

"Oh, that's right," he said, without much concern. Then he walked over to the other side of the roof, which faced Amsterdam Street, and began to study the tops of the trees in Parque México that were visible above the rooftops.

Galo felt more and more confused. He was gazing at the city with this man who did not speak like a Mexican and was possibly there to kill him so he could begin the work of conquering humanity's greatest treasure. "Does he know," thought Galo, "that beneath this water tank I keep all the stories this street needs to keep working? Does he know that I would be willing to push him right now so he falls and dies just to make sure that the world doesn't miss its chance to become better?"

Aloud, Galo said, "You are not Mexican."

"No."

"Where are you from?"

"Argentina."

"Like Carlos Gardel."

"You know Gardel?" He seemed surprised.

"Yes, since I was young. My father used to listen to him every day."

The man smiled. He inhaled and closed his eyes. "Return, with a wrinkled forehead," he sang, very much out of tune, "the snow over time . . . settled on my temples."

Galo remained silent for a moment, staring intently at the man's chest, while the man himself looked towards Chapultepec Castle.

"It sounds strange, when you breathe."

"A little," he replied indifferently, as he stretched his arms up towards the sky.

"What are you doing in Mexico?"

"I studied what could be done to cure asthma. That's why I cannot breathe, because of the asthma. That's why I want the cats."

"Is that all?"

"What do you mean 'Is that all'?"

"All you want here in Mexico. You aren't interested in anything else?"

"Ah."

"And what about . . ." Galo finally plucked up the courage to ask, "what's inside those suitcases?"

"They're for hunting cats," said the man, and then roared with laughter.

Galo's face remained serious.

"I'm sorry, it was a joke; but don't worry, nobody ever laughs at my jokes. Are you afraid of guns?"

"I'm afraid of what you will do with them."

The man's large, square forehead crumpled into a frown.

"And how do you know what we want to do?"

Galo said nothing. He looked steadily back at the man, his expression worried but firm. He knew that the most important moment of his life had arrived. The man couldn't see it, but at that very moment Galo was being wrapped in a flag, and he could feel it upon his shoulders. He squeezed his fists shut. He was ready for anything. The man, on the other hand, breathed in and out several times, slowly. He hesitated for a moment as if, Galo thought, he was proposing a ceasefire with the cats so that they wouldn't start meowing then and there.

"All right, let's try something. First of all, you have no reason to be afraid of me."

"Are you going to try and conquer the street? Is that why you came to my house?"

The man looked into Galo's eyes, first the left and then the right, as if he was searching for something else in or behind them, as if eyes could explain more clearly than words. He didn't find what he was looking for, but he felt as though he could speak honestly with the boy. Meanwhile, Galo felt that a potent force was growing in his arms and seemed to be saying "Push him off, now that he's not expecting it!"

"All right. If you explain to me why you are afraid we will conquer the street, I will tell you why the suitcases are filled with guns." And then he added, "Trust me, because I am going to trust you."

The man sat down with his legs crossed, one on top of the other, his feet pulled up over his thighs, and waited. Galo took a few minutes to reflect on the situation. Finally he decided that the time had come to tell the truth. He couldn't turn back now. If he was facing the very enemy he had been waiting for, that enemy wouldn't be telling him anything he didn't already know, and perhaps Galo would be able to convince him to change his mind.

He began to speak with great care, calculating the meaning of each word as he uttered it. It was the first time he had had the courage to tell anybody all he had learned. Gradually, as his story continued, the penetrating gaze of the man before him, who gave him his full attention throughout, made Galo feel more sure of himself. The flag around him loosened and began to fall off until his muscles were rid of the tension that had hardened them. He told the man how he had discovered, several years ago, that Amsterdam Street was the place where the world's time was born, and this was why it was humanity's greatest treasure. As soon as he had realized this truth, Galo told the man, he understood that somebody had to take responsibility for looking after the street, because if it fell into the hands of people like the President of the United States, or the ex-president Cárdenas, or Hitler, who was perhaps at that very moment thawing out or had done so already, or Franco, then things would get even worse than they already were, because they would be able to make more cities disappear under gigantic mushrooms and make many more men watch as their mothers' eyes were pulled out, and all of those were things that he knew had happened in the world recently, and he also told him that he had been chosen by destiny to look after Amsterdam Street: this was why his father had built him a chair on which he could sit and learn how to be nothing because he hadn't been able to learn how to be a carpenter; this was why his bougainvillea kept growing, following the strings and the nails that he added to the wall every spring; this was why he did not leave his house, because all of those things were fundamental to his being the street's guardian, and he also told him that, for the very same reason, even before he knew that he had to dedicate his life to protecting humanity's greatest treasure, he had been collecting a few of the memories of the men who could have ended up dead, burned, or thrown onto the trash heaps in many of Europe's cities and towns. And after saying these things and seeing that the man seemed increasingly enthusiastic, he showed him the packages of hair belonging to Garfias the poet and Rabbi Cann and Morlans the Catalan and Lindberg the violinist, and he told him that these memories were what the street needed to keep generating humanity's true time; and not just that, he also told him that Galo's father, before slipping the black comb into his back pocket, listened to Carlos Gardel every morning after Toño Bermúdez's morning news bulletin while he sawed, sanded, and varnished dozens and dozens of pieces of wood that filled the air with the smell of resin, until one day he left with the woman with the blue eyes for whom he had been waiting for a long time, and that that was the fault of General Cárdenas, whose moustache Galo had cut off one afternoon as vengeance for what he had done, just the thing Clodomiro Santibáñez would have loved to do to Franco, the same Mr. Santibáñez who had taught him that the church was the scum of the earth and so many other things, because he was his assistant and apprentice, and he also told him about Ana's grandfather, who lost the perfume factory because of Hitler and who still now, undoubtedly, was looking for a place where he could tie his sheet, hang himself, and keep fighting his invisible enemies for eternity, and about Mr. Franz Weill, who came running to the office one day holding a piece of paper covered in stamps as if it were a flag blowing in the wind, and he also told him about Ana, who was a murderer because she had killed Christ and was the only woman he had ever kissed. . . . And just like this, as the hours passed there on the roof of his house, next to the packages filled with memories, Galo told the stranger the story of his entire life, this man who breathed as though he had ten cats inside his lungs and who might be a soldier of the large army that wanted to conquer Amsterdam Street.

"And if necessary, I am willing to defend the street by wrapping my body in a flag and throwing myself off this building and down onto the pavement, because I will never allow it to fall into the hands of the enemy," Galo said in conclusion and, feeling more tired than he had ever felt, because he had never spoken uninterrupted for such a long time, he sat down and closed his eyes for a moment.

＝

The man had listened with the utmost attention, his eyes fixed on Galo's without blinking. He was profoundly moved.

He stood up. He walked away from Galo and stood with his back turned and was silent for a few minutes, trying to absorb all the information he had just heard. Meanwhile, he watched as the sun struck the volcanoes' slopes head on.

"Now it's your turn," said Galo, using that time to recover. "Tell me what the guns are for."

The man turned to look at him, serious, excited. His eyes were shining. And with the same seriousness and excitement with which Galo had told him his secret, as if after a long search he had finally found the person he needed to talk to, the person who would understand him completely, he told him this:

"We are going to use them to change the world."

28

THERE, ON THE ROOF of his house, while they waited for the cats to appear, the man had told Galo that, with the guns inside the suitcases, the man with ten cats in his lungs and his friends were going to board a ship, they were going to travel to an island, and they were going to begin to change the world.

"We are getting ready," he told him. "We are collecting more weapons. We are waiting for our leader to tell us when we must leave and board a ship. We move between houses over and over again because the people who want to stop us from changing the world are chasing us, and that's why we need to be here in your house, waiting until they tell us the time has come. Meanwhile, I will keep collecting cats to see if I can find the cure to this damn disease that won't let me breathe."

A meow interrupted them.

The man, a tiger, jumped on top of the cat, caught it, and stuffed it into a bag. It struggled desperately inside but eventually went still.

It was getting dark. They had spent the entire day on the roof, waiting for the cats and talking. They didn't feel hungry or thirsty.

"There are many people who want to change the world, Galo, but they do not know how to do it, or they have already failed. We are really going to do it. We are going to do whatever is necessary to make the world a different place."

While the man was explaining, Galo realized that they had chosen his house to hide in because only on Amsterdam Street should something so important begin.

"How do you change the world?"

"You start a revolution."

"How do you start a revolution?"

This time, the meow was coming from the roof of a neighbouring house. The man crept towards it, hopped over the dividing wall and approached the cat. With each step he took, the cat retreated a little. When he felt he was at a reasonable distance, he launched himself at it, stretching his body mid-air, as though he were a tiger, a hawk; but his attempt was futile. The cat jumped up onto the water tank and looked down indifferently at the man, who picked himself up from the ground as if nothing had happened, as if he hadn't just smashed into the cement. The cat looked at him as if wanting to say that he would never be able to beat it, but the man did not give up; he responded to the cat's provocation with the threatening look of a tiger willing to do whatever it took to catch its prey, as if catching the cat was the most important thing he would ever do in all his life, as if the cat's gaze left him no other choice and was forcing him to fight over and over again until he could defeat it. He jumped with all his strength and almost grabbed hold of one of its legs, but it escaped once again. The cat's meows became increasingly agitated. Its tail, tense, flicked from one side to the other, its eyes trained on the man's every movement. He was once again in attack position, his arms stretched out to his sides to make the cat feel smaller, cornered, in a battle it had never imagined or sought out, which seemed not only to be about settling the issue of whether man or cat was superior but, due to its opponent's absolute determination, also seemed to hold the key to the world's fate.

Galo watched from the roof of his own house: the adversaries were bathed in moonlight. He felt that with every passing second their lives depended on their agility and whether they were cunning enough to guess what the other's next move would be. Suddenly the cats inside the man's lungs began to meow furiously, as though compelling him to be more agile, stronger, more stubborn than the cat before him.

Almost at midnight, after the epic battle had come to an end and the cat dozed next to its captive companion inside the bag, Galo asked, "What is revolution?"

"A figure with no outline, that's revolution," the man replied, tired, victorious:

It's a vacuum . . .

It's a flowing river . . .

It is not pleasant, but it will never cease to be useful . . .

With a revolution there are three kinds of men: the timid one who doesn't see it; the coward who laughs at it; the brave one who starts it . . .

It is the great mystery of the world. The value of words depends upon revolution, that which rewards itself for noble actions and punishes itself for evil ones . . .

It is life. It is soft and hot, because softness and heat is the nature of life: the living man is soft and hot, the dead man is hard and cold . . .

Revolution is fury, Galo. It is tender fury.

===

They were quiet for a long time. They looked up at the stars. The man smoked a cigarette. Afterwards he asked Galo to tell him a little more about Ana.

They came down from the roof just as the sun started to come up. The contours of the volcanoes against the sky were infinitely precise on the horizon. El Ajusco re-emerged from inside the fog and, closer to them, the first rays of sunshine hit the tops of the tallest trees in Parque México. There were four cats inside the bag.

They went their separate ways with a hug by the bougainvillea.

"I need to ask you a favour."

"Anything at all, Galo."

He woke up at midday. He went to the bathroom to wash his body. First his right arm, then his left, then his neck. Once he was finished he dried himself off and came out into the patio. At that moment he realized that the door to the large room was wide open. He poked his head inside. There was nothing there. The small room was empty too. The only remaining trace of the tenants was a small hardcover book, a little bundle of hair, and the cats, still trapped inside the bag.

29

M ORE THAN A YEAR had passed, and the letter had no
return address on it. It was inside an envelope that
somebody had slipped underneath the door.

Galo could read it because a few months earlier something
very important had occurred in the city, which he believed himself to have caused, that had made such an impact on him that it
forced him to learn how to read.

It happened during a period in which his mother had
decided to stop renting out the rooms and instead use them to
set up her own business. She opened an ice cream parlour called
Nueva Michoacán, which she left him in charge of.

Galo had had a very distressing dream the night it happened.
He dreamed that he heard shouts coming from the patio and
left his room to see what was going on. He saw his father, standing on top of his chair, sawing off the strongest branches of the
bougainvillea. Next to him was the woman with the burning
blue embers, desperately searching for the hand that his mother
had sawn off. She couldn't find it because the floor was completely covered in the plant's leaves, flowers, and branches. The
ground opened up mouths all over the patio so that it could

eat. Both of them were crying. Galo woke up as he was about to wrap his arms around his father, as he attempted to tell him, although the words refused to come out of his mouth, that the hand wasn't there because his father and the woman had already taken it themselves.

Since he couldn't get back to sleep, he decided to get up and go up to the roof. The moon was bright that night. After looking towards the street and feeling the silence wrap itself around him, he lay down with his back against the cement, stretched his arms out from his sides in order to allow the cold to slowly creep up and seize his body. He focused on one star. He stopped blinking.

He decided: "If I don't take my eyes off that star for a single second until the sun comes up, my father will come back . . ." and the effort he made to keep his eyes on that star was so great that the earth began to shake, and it shook harder than it ever had before, but Galo didn't take his eyes off the star and so it shook even harder, and the earth trembled so powerfully that all the city's buildings swayed, and many people came out of their houses on Amsterdam Street shouting and crying, and sirens could be heard coming from all directions, and Galo's mother also came out of her room in great distress, but despite all the noise and crying and collapsing buildings, Galo's father did not appear.

The following day, after opening the ice cream parlour, he switched on the radio to listen to Toño Bermúdez and found out that the sculpture of a giant winged woman had crashed to the ground thanks to him.

That morning he made a deal with a man, who every day would buy a double cone with two scoops of chocolate and vanilla, to teach Galo how to read in exchange for free ice cream.

Galo wanted to learn for two reasons: so he could understand what the newspapers were saying about the woman with the

wings who had fallen because of him, and so he could read the
hardback book his friend had left him along with the bag of cats.

A MOUNTAIN. DECEMBER 1957

Dear Galo:

*I didn't get the chance to say goodbye. An hour after we parted
ways on the patio, we received the order to leave. But I want
you to know that I will consider you my best friend for the rest
of my life.*

*I don't know what will happen to me. I am in the middle
of a jungle that treats the "cats inside my lungs" very badly
indeed, but for now I am coping.*

*Things are not as easy as we thought they would be, although
I have to admit I am happy. This is what I wanted, what I
have been searching for without realizing for a very long time.*

*In any case, I am sure that we are getting closer and closer
to winning.*

And afterwards? I don't know.

*The Revolution, this deep and mysterious river, this
dizzying abyss, creates itself without caring much about what
it does to us: nobody knows when it might suck you dry (and
when that happens, what does one become?), nor which way
the current will flow.*

*On the scarce occasions that I have had time, I think about
you a great deal, about the enormous treasure you must protect.*

Don't give up!

SO LONG, FRIEND.

Galo was never able to resolve either of these two reasons. By the time he learned to read, the newspapers were no longer publishing articles about the angel woman's fall. He had to settle for what he heard on the radio and the comments people made when they came to buy ice cream.

He didn't get to read the book either, because when he went to look for it he discovered it was no longer there. One afternoon his mother came across him desperately searching the house. He had already rummaged through the kitchen shelves, the wardrobe, and even the trash. She asked him what he was looking for, and when he said a small hardback book, she told him she had thrown it out along with the bag that had contained the cats.

30

OCCUPIED WITH HIS reading lessons and selling ice cream, Galo was able to forget about his mission for a while. As long as his mother wasn't trying to rent out the rooms, he had no reason to worry. Once every two or three days he would go up to the roof to check that the packages of hair were still in good condition. He had to repack fourteen of them, because for a stretch of time, a few cats had chosen the area underneath the water tank to urinate, and the newspaper had begun to rot.

As a result of his new situation, he was able to learn very important things. For example, he learned that the person who asked for ice cream was not the same as the person who preferred sorbet, and that the man who liked chocolate was very different from the one who chose lime. For some reason the fat women took a lot longer to choose than the thin ones. With men it was different: they almost always had already made up their minds before they walked inside. At the very most they might deliberate between two options, but no more.

Why were people's tastes so different? Why did single women prefer fruit-flavoured ice cream, and why were the dark-coloured ice creams so popular with young boys? Why on sunny days did the Jews always choose vanilla but the Spaniards tamarind or soursop? On rainy days, what made tall men ask for strawberry and pregnant women café au lait? Happy faces: greens and yellows; worried faces: red and browns; hurried faces: lime or chocolate . . . and eventually the time came when Galo was able to guess what people were going to choose. When a woman came into Nueva Michoacán carrying market bags at midday, he peeled the lid off the guava sorbet. If two boys came in, each one angry with the other, he would prepare one chocolate and one strawberry. And the clients expressed their gratitude with a smile. "How did you know what I wanted?" they would ask, and Galo would say things like, "Well it's just that I saw you getting out of the taxi in a hurry," or "you sighed as you watched Mr. Gumaro's daughter cross the road," because Galo grew to understand his clients' tastes the same way he had learned everything else in his life: by closely observing every movement, every look, every hand gesture, every laugh, and even every word that had been left unspoken. He also learned that the decision of which ice cream to ask for depended not only on the characteristics of each person but also on unforeseen circumstances. He realized that if Mr. José Prudencio Aguirre, who normally asked for a scoop of lime and a scoop of blackberry on humid days, had to adjust his hat just before coming in because a gust of wind had taken him by surprise and displaced it, he would instead ask for two scoops of strawberry, and if Rosalinda's mother didn't look at her lovingly before opening the door then she wouldn't want the combination of vanilla and sweetcorn but would ask for grape. The smallest surprise, an unexpected look, a dog barking, a car braking abruptly, a leaf falling from the ash tree in front of the ice cream parlour, changed people's minds. And

Galo had to learn all of this in order to better serve his clients. "This change in people, this is also part of the true human time that Amsterdam Street measures," Galo thought. And just as Mr. Clodomiro Santibáñez's hairdresser's shop had helped him to learn so much about men, the ice-cream parlour taught him that it wasn't only size, sex, or age that defined his clients and made them choose one flavour over another, but that the choice was also influenced by the subtle changes in their mood caused by events that happened suddenly, at any time, and which they could do nothing to avoid.

A man walks slowly along Amsterdam Street. His eyes are fixed on something in the distance. His legs seem determined to take him to a particular place. Suddenly, something unexpected happens: Mrs. Violeta Horcasitas emerges from her house, ready to take her dog for a walk just as she does every morning at that precise time. The first thing the dog sees upon leaving his house are the man's legs. He barks because he is startled. The man does a little jump to one side, led by his instinct for survival. Mrs. Horcasitas tugs on her dog's leash and apologizes, embarrassed. The man, whose eyes are trained on the dog at that moment, looks up and sees the woman. First he sees her eyes; Mrs. Horcasitas' eyes say something to him that he can't quite put his finger on but that immediately awakens the memory of a garden: a house with a garden. The house he lived in until he was seven. The memory suddenly fills him with a sweet nostalgia. He then discovers Mrs. Horcasitas' lips. They say something. He wouldn't be able to explain it, but they remind him of the rumble of the waves the last time he went on holiday to the beach. And the hands. And the dress. And the tone of Mrs. Horcasitas' voice as she says, "I'm sorry." The dog now wants to go over to the ash tree in front of the Nueva Michoacán ice cream parlour. Mrs. Horcasitas feels an insistent tug on the hand holding the leash. She smiles at the man, as if the smile were a goodbye and one last apology and she crosses in front of him in order to get to the tree. Now the dog pees, lifting one of his back legs. The man continues walking. Mrs. Horcasitas turns to look at the man's back as he gets farther away. Then she moves in the opposite direction. Two steps later, the man who seven seconds earlier had seen Acapulco's Horno beach and the garden of the house he grew up in with a strange intensity, turns, without knowing the reason. He doesn't know why, but he wants to see Mrs. Horcasitas again. He sees her back. He doesn't know why, but he feels profoundly frustrated. He thinks: "Why doesn't she turn to look at me?" When he starts walking again, Galo, who has seen everything from the ice cream parlour, realizes that neither the way he looks nor the way he walks are the same anymore. Something has been forever disrupted in that man's life. Twenty minutes later, Mrs. Horcasitas returns with her dog because the morning walk is over. As always, she comes into the ice cream parlour, but instead of asking for the walnut ice cream she has asked for every morning since the store opened, she asks for guava sorbet.

———

Did Ana kill Jesus Christ because he didn't follow God's laws, or because of that afternoon at school when three girls circled her and shouted the last verse of the Hitler Youth anthem? Did his mother saw off the hand of the woman with the trunk because she saw how the woman was embracing her husband or because earlier that day a vendor had stolen a kilo of green beans from her? Did Franz Weill take Mr. Gueiser's perfumery because they gave him a piece of paper covered in stamps or because he had dreamed the night before that he would propose to his girlfriend and marry her the following summer? Did the man who had written Galo a letter saying he would be his best friend forever want to start a revolution because he wanted to change the world or because the desperate and ferocious meowing of the ten cats inside his lungs left him no other option?

Why do the things that happen happen? Why do people do the things they do? Can anyone ever really know? Do we need to know? If a leaf falling from a tree, an unexpected look, a gust of wind, can make people change their mind about what ice cream they want, Galo asked himself, if their desires are so fragile, then what makes everything appear so organized, as if everyone knew the direction their life would take and the destiny that awaits them?

31

AT THE BEGINNING OF 1967, Galo's mother was in an
accident on the corner of Amsterdam and Sonora that
paralyzed her legs.

She had to sell the market stall, close Nueva Michoacán,
and rent out the rooms again. She opted for a reliable income
from rent over the small amount of money she received incon-
sistently from the ice cream parlour.

Galo resented the new situation because, instead of being
able to keep thinking about his recent discoveries, his fears
about the tenants returned, and due to his mother's physical
state he had to help her get up, go to bed, and bathe. Every
morning he would lift her into her wheelchair and take her to
the bathroom. He would wait by the door until she told him
she was finished, and then he would take her out and bring her
to the kitchen or back to bed, depending on her mood. Then he
had to dry the chair, which was always wet. On top of all of this,
every afternoon his mother would ask him to give her massages
and apply ointments to relieve the abrasions and blisters that
were slowly corroding the skin on her back and legs.

While he did this, the mother would whisper over and over,
"Guardian angel, my spiritual guide, whom I have disappointed

countless times with my sins, and chased away with my crimes, do not abandon me; I beg you, in the midst of danger; do not withdraw your support; do not leave me exposed and vulnerable to the shots of an enemy as astute as he is cruel; do not let me out of your sight for even a moment, but allow your loving inspirations to lead and strengthen my soul; revive my weak and almost-still heart, because it is without love; send it just one spark of the soft, pure flames that envelop you, so that when the end of this short and miserable life comes, I can attain eternal life in your company and of all the angels', and see Jesus, my Redeemer, forevermore, love him, praise him and bless him. So be it." And if she still felt Galo's hands on her body, she would repeat the necessary Hail Marys until he was finished.

Although he had shared a bed and a room with his mother for so many years, this was the first time he had seen and touched his mother's body.

This wrinkled and brittle skin, Galo thought one afternoon, as he spread the oily paste he scooped from the jars across her body, this sore skin, covered in blisters, this fetid skin, is my mother's skin, but it is also a woman's skin. Why do I not feel, when I touch her, the same way I felt when I touched Ana's skin? Their bodies are not the same, but not because one is wrinkly or covered in blisters. They are not the same because I do not feel the same when I touch them. Encouraged by the steady whispers of his mother, who despite being extremely uncomfortable was lying down on her back, fingering the beads of a rosary, Galo remembered just then that the priest had said that all men were equal in the eyes of God. And men were bodies.

Only God can say that all men are equal, and He can only say this because He has never touched them. If you do not touch, you do not feel, and if you do not feel, you cannot distinguish.

Poor God, he thought finally, while his mother repented before her guardian angel, you have made infinite bodies but are not able to tell the difference between them. This must have been why God was so sad.

32

D ESPITE ALL HIS new daily tasks, Galo felt relaxed; nothing had happened to put in danger the treasure he was guarding so carefully, not for years.

The mother bore her circumstances with resignation, thanks in part to the fact that, ever since the accident, the priest began to visit her at home every morning to make sure the woman was fulfilling her commitments to God.

One day, after her confession, he told her that he was beginning to worry about her future. "You are growing old, and now with your disability I am even more concerned. It is true that Galo helps you a little, but being the way he is you can't rely on him much, and at this stage I don't know what he could do to help you once your body fails you," he said. "You need to take precautions. As time goes on you will receive less and less money for those little rooms that hardly anybody wants anymore, and then what will you do?"

Before marrying Galo's father, the couple had only decided they could start a family after he received an unexpected inheritance from an uncle. The future mother lived in a small town near the city of Morelia. Her parents were farmers and since their only daughter had moved to the city, they eventually sold their land and spent their final years living in the house of a good friend. This meant that Galo's mother had nothing except for the house, and her son.

She had done well to stop her husband from taking Galo with him. After all, her son may not have been quite right in the head, but he had been good company, and despite not ever leaving the house and spending most of his time sitting in the chair his father had made, he was a hard worker. What did it matter if he wasn't like everyone else, if he was thirty-four years old and hadn't yet gotten married, or if he hadn't been inside a church since he was five? "Now that my legs don't work," the woman thought, "I'm grateful he doesn't like to leave the house, because he looks after me, and he will always look after me. I haven't had such bad luck after all. My husband may have left me, but I cannot complain. I have had a few men, I have been very faithful to my lord Jesus Christ, and I have always had enough to eat. What more could one ask for?"

But the priest had sowed the seeds of doubt, and in a way he was right: over the years those rooms had gradually deteriorated, and new modern buildings had sprung up in the neighbourhood that had better spaces for corner stores and any other kind of business.

"A few days ago an engineer came to see me in the parish church and asked me to help him find a plot of land for a new building," the priest told her. "You ought to think about it. With the money he would pay you, you could live comfortably for the rest of your life in one of those cozy apartments and even pay somebody to look after you."

"What about Galo?" asked the woman.

"I can make sure he is looked after. If you like I could speak with the bishop to see that he gets accepted into a convent, since they are always in need of people to help with cleaning and the rest of it. Besides, remember that since your poor son is the way he is, it will be much easier for him to get into heaven and avoid getting stuck in limbo if he is living in a convent." The mother told the priest she would think about it.

One night while they were eating she asked him, "Galo, my son, what will you do once I am dead? Who will look after you?"

"You will be alive for many more years to come."

"That's in the hands of the Lord," the mother replied, "and I am afraid of what might happen to you."

They never spoke about it again, but Galo was left feeling worried.

What was death? Until now, it had been something that happened far away: A rope, a tree, and Mr. Lindberg's sister and father dead. A plane, an order, and two cities dead. Could death one day come to Amsterdam Street and into his house? Was death something that turned up without warning, like the small things that happened to his clients in the ice cream parlour, those insignificant details like putting a black comb in a back pocket, like raising and lowering your arms in front of a man with a moustache who ranted to a crowd? Would death eventually paralyze the healthy parts of his mother's body, until she was left completely inert?

And just as his mother could die, might he, the guardian of Amsterdam Street, die too? Who would look after human time once he was gone? What was the point, Galo asked himself, of watching over it now if one day he would be dead?

"While I remain alive, I guard it because that's what I am supposed to do. Once I am dead, what good will it do to have been the guardian?" he thought. The only solution Galo could come up with was to never die. He had to be eternal. Eternal, just like Amsterdam Street must be.

33

GALO RECEIVED another letter at the end of September. It had been ten years since he had received the first.

Who am I, Galo? What is this thin, dirty body, eaten away by so many mosquito bites? What are these tired lungs, which never learned how to breathe?

I am hungry, Galo. It has been a lifetime since I ate a decent piece of meat. I am tired. I don't know how many nights it has been since I last slept.

I am furious. Nothing went how I thought it would. Nothing is how it should be. Nothing is what it should have been. I wasn't what I wanted to be. I always had to leave where I had been because nobody would listen to me, because my words did not speak to anyone.

Have my words ever spoken to anyone? Has anyone ever listened to me? And what would have happened if they had? Nothing Galo, nothing would have happened. Man is what he is. And I never knew what he was. I don't know it, now that I am hungry, now that I am so tired, now that I can barely breathe, and I didn't know it before.

Can history be erased? Can everything that has happened up until now be forgotten? Can the course be altered? Can somebody stop the inexorable advance of darkness in the world, forever?

I am going to die, Galo, and I do not care. I wouldn't know how or why to keep on living. I am going to die, and I have done nothing. I am going to die because my body is nothing but a wheezing lump, because I couldn't even beat these cats that got into my lungs and started scratching at the inside walls of my body with their claws, again and again, that tore my flesh to ribbons, that mocked my steps. "I want, I want, I want," I would say. "We won't allow it," they would reply.

What are these cats, Galo, that have, I am now sure of it, beaten me? What would I have been without them, without them scratching and destroying?

I was capricious, because I thought that life was like a movie. Gardel playing a guitar and singing, a smile on his face, his eyes half-closed, gazing at the lights of Buenos Aires from a boat's prow.

Why was I capricious? Why did I think that life was a movie? Because I didn't realize that I would end up here, alone, tired, hungry, and that there is nothing about a dream that could ever be real.

The Revolution starts itself. The Revolution is an insatiable abyss. The Revolution is my lungs that never fill with air. The Revolution doesn't exist. The Revolution is not The Revolution. The Revolution eats The Revolution. The Revolution is me, now. The Revolution is hungry. The Revolution is tired.

Who can see me, Galo? Who can see me, here, now, Galo? Who will know that here is where my body has ended up?

I am alone, and nobody can see me, Galo. I am alone in the middle of a crowd of eyes that do not see me. The world, Galo, will keep turning, and I am going to die.

In the city of Prague, one night a long time ago, I fell in love with a woman. It was very cold. I left the hotel where I was staying, and my eyes found hers. A moment. Three seconds.

Everything I used to believe in dissolved in those three seconds. Every one of my convictions was met with doubt and dissipated in those three seconds. Those three seconds spent looking at her were enough to know that I had never loved and would never love another woman.

And there, on that street in Prague, that night, looking at those singular eyes, I knew everything I needed to know. Also that today, here, now, I would be dying.

If three seconds was enough to fall in love with that woman, how many did it take for me to decide that today, here, I would be dying?

Those who might occasionally remember me will think that I died for The Revolution. I am no longer sure, Galo, perhaps I am dying because I did not dare to face the vertigo of the other, deeper chasm that opened before me when I saw those singular eyes, that night in Prague, for three seconds.

Is it always like this, Galo? Do we always die because of something we were not aware was killing us? Will we always live for something that we were not aware was keeping us alive?

Immediately after finishing it, Galo read it a second time, this letter sent to him by the man who had promised to be his friend forever, the man who had given him a little bit of his hair hours before boarding a ship to go start changing the world on an island, and who was now telling him that he was beginning to be dead. This was why a few days later, when the man's photo appeared in El Excélsior, smiling, eyes open, Galo was sure that his friend had finally finished dying, and that the ten cats that used to meow inside his lungs had escaped a few seconds before, and that was why his mouth was slightly open.

The night of October 11, 1967, Galo went up to the roof and re-wrapped his friend's hair in the sheet of newspaper in which the photo of him had appeared, reclined and smiling, his mouth slightly open, resting and no longer hungry and without the claws inside him that had scratched him his entire life and used to tell him "we won't allow it" even though he would shout "I want, I want, I want."

34

TODAY THERE IS a great silence over the earth, a great silence — and stillness, a great stillness, because the King sleeps. God slept in the flesh and raised up those who were sleeping from the ages . . . Truly He goes to seek out our first parent like a lost sheep.

I command you: Awake, sleeper! I have not made you to be held prisoner in the underworld. Arise from the dead; I am the life of the dead.

"Where is my father?" Galo asked himself. Is he in a city in the United States sawing planks of wood and filling the air with the smell of resin, to be inhaled by the woman with the blue eyes? Does he listen to Gardel? Does he keep the orange measuring tape in his back-left pocket? Is the red-and-blue pencil tucked behind his left ear?

And what if he were walking along Amsterdam Street, covered in rags, blind, desperately searching for the front door of the house? Shouldn't Galo go out and look for him, as though he really were a lost sheep? Shouldn't Galo visit those who live in the darkness and shadows of death?

Galo looked after his mother, he took her to the bathroom, he prepared her food, and he thought about his father.

He thought about his father, he thought about death, and that is how he spent his days until a couple came to the house looking to rent the rooms. They were students.

They knocked on the door a few months after his friend had finished dying in a photo in the newspaper. It was August 6, 1968, and Galo knew that was the date because when they arrived he was listening to Toño Bermúdez on the radio saying that on a day like today, twenty-three years ago, in less than a minute, ten square kilometres of the city of Hiroshima was turned to dust, along with the bodies of 78,150 people.

—————

"Isabel studies biology, and I study film," Leonardo told him, after Galo showed them the rooms and said how much the rent was.

"We both study at the university, and although it's far away from here we like this street and we like the rooms and we can pay," Isabel said. "I am going to have a baby in five months or so and that's why we want to live together. We would be in the big room and we would put a crib in the little one for our child," Isabel said as she happily walked through the rooms, one hand trailing along the walls behind her while the other rested on her belly.

"We are going to call him Ernesto Emiliano. His name will be Ernesto Emiliano Domínguez Ciprián, or if it's a girl her name will be Ernestina Emiliana Domínguez Ciprián.

"Every night we will read the baby a poem before bedtime; that way its little body will absorb them while it's dreaming so that when it's born it will have more poems inside it than bones.

"Leonardo is going to make great films; he will be the best film director in Mexico and one of the most important directors in the world. I am going to study the theory of evolution because even though I am only in the fourth semester of my degree, I already know that that theory doesn't make sense. It's a trick, all this about living beings evolving. It's not true and I will prove it. Do you understand Galo? They wanted to make us believe that living beings evolve, instead of revolt. This is why I will study until I can demonstrate it's a lie, and this is why Leonardo will make films too, to prove to everyone that just by making films and revealing evolution to be a lie we can change the world.

"Can we stay here?"

Galo told them they could, because he already knew how important it was to people like them, who wanted to change the world, to be able to start doing it from within the heart of Amsterdam Street, and because as he listened he watched Isabel's hands carefully and he saw that they were soft and warm like Ana's; and lastly because he knew he would enjoy listening to the poems they read to their child.

35

A FEW WEEKS HAD gone by since they had rented the rooms. One day Isabel and Leonardo took chairs out to the sidewalk to sit by the front door. Isabel was convinced that getting some sunshine would be good for her son or daughter, regardless of the fact the baby was still inside her belly. Galo had sat down by the entrance to listen to the poem that Isabel had prepared, and then Antonio Garfias walked past, who by then had become a very old man, and he too stopped to listen.

the breach in the horizon
the cynocephalus
let the lotus bearer of the world come
the pearly upheaval of dolphins
cracking the shell of the sea
let a plunge of islands come
let it come from the disappearing of days of dead
flesh in the quicklime of birds of prey
let the ovaries of the water come where the future stirs its testicles
let the wolves come who feed in the untamed openings of the body at
the hour when my moon and your sun meet at the ecliptic inn

under the reserve of my uvula there is a wallow of boars
under the grey stone of the day there are your eyes which are a shim-
mering conglomerate of coccinella
in the glance of disorder there is this swallow of mint and broom
which melts always to be reborn in the tidal wave of your light
Calm and lull oh my voice the child who does not know that the map
of spring is always to be drawn again

Isabel soothed the child inside her belly with her voice while Leonardo's right hand slowly rubbed her back, following, Galo thought, a map only he knew existed, and Galo allowed himself to be soothed by the poem too.

When Isabel finished reading, Antonio Garfias approached and said he would be prepared to do anything for them, because he had often seen how the spring tried to restore itself between his hands and he didn't know how or why it had wilted again and again, and now, seeing that a man and a woman could still sit down outside to read a book by the great Césaire, he had realized that all was not lost.

And Galo, who had heard that man bemoan the distance that separated him from his country so many times, realized that there, in the very same place where he had seen the trees grow, the ones he didn't love because they weren't the ones he'd seen as a child, Garfias's words had moved Isabel and Leonardo because they asked for more, they wanted him to keep talking because it did them good and it gave them the strength to keep going, and so Garfias told them about how in Madrid and Barcelona, where — while they kept fighting to defend the last stone, and the Nationalists were dropping bombs and burning everything down — they never stopped singing and reciting songs and poems, and a few hours later, when the sky had clouded over and the rain was about to fall, the two students, Isabel and Leonardo, invited Garfias to come inside to their rooms so they could keep talking, and once they were there, while the poet's gaze ran along the bookshelves where Isabel had arranged the books she planned to read to her child, Leonardo, serious, after closing the door so that Galo's mother wouldn't hear them, told Antonio Garfias that if he really wanted to do something for them he would teach them how to make Molotov cocktails.

====

And this was how Galo came to see, watching from the window, that after returning from where they learned how to make films and prove that the theory of evolution was a great lie, they would make many Molotov cocktails, one after another, and every night before going to sleep they would read poetry so that Ernesto Emiliano or Ernestina Emiliana would have more poems than bones.

And this was how one morning at dawn Galo saw Isabel and Leonardo leave and meet with other young people like them on the corner, and they took with them all the Molotov cocktails they had made, as well as thousands of pieces of paper they planned to hand out, on which was written in red and black ink the words "Socialism or Death! Long live the Proletarian Vanguard! Join us! For two, three, many more Vietnams!" and Galo had gone up to the roof to watch them, because the previous afternoon they had told him that they would begin to change the world that morning, and that in order to change it they had to burn down the city and hand out those pieces of paper so that the People would read them, because after reading them they would understand that The Revolution was just, The Revolution started itself, and all the things Galo's only friend had explained to him, and that the People, after reading their pieces of paper, would follow them, would run with them and·burn the city with them, until the fire consumed the army's trucks and the government buildings, and the president would say, "All right, they beat me; you are stronger and fiercer, and the People ran and burned the city by your side."

And although he stayed up on the roof all day long watching the street he didn't hear anything about them or about the world beginning to change, until that night when Leonardo returned, arms bleeding, dazed, running, shouting, crying, nose black and mangled, missing a shoe, and he hid underneath the bed and didn't stop shouting and crying until seven men arrived and broke down the door, and while Galo's mother shouted from her bed, unaware of what was happening inside the rooms, they pulled him out from under the bed, and although he bit them and tried to violently shake them off they pushed him inside a car while he shouted: "Tell me where you took my Isabel! Tell me what you did with her and my son! Tell me, please, tell me!"

And Galo, that night, after telling his mother what had happened and giving her a painkiller because she was very agitated and she would have never been able to sleep in that state, realized that Isabel would not be able to prove that the theory of evolution was a great lie, and that Leonardo would not make the best movies in the world, and that nobody, absolutely nobody came out of their houses to see what was happening to Leonardo, not a single person on Amsterdam Street even opened their window.

36

ONE OF THE FIRST nights of the winter of 1970 Galo
dreamed that he left the house and that on one corner
he bumped into Ana's father, and on another into God.
He found Ana's father lying naked on the pavement, his
head propped up against a tree. Galo asked him what he was
doing there, and the man told him he was resting because the
journey to Guadalajara had worn him out. Galo asked him
about Ana, and the man told him she couldn't come and visit
him because she had to help her grandfather find a good place
to tie his sheet. Galo thought about telling him that Hitler was
frozen and could return at any moment, but a desperate wail
made him turn towards the very end of the street, where an old,
skinny, weak man was leaning against a wall, trying to hold himself up. He looked like Rabbi Cann, although he was much taller.

Galo went towards him, knowing that the old man he was
approaching was God. He was weeping, clearly in great distress.
By His feet two cats were licking the floor, lapping up His fallen
tears. In that moment he thought that God was crying because
He could not wake up His son, the one He had gone down to
search for among the dead, but God told him that it was not
that: He cried because He had lost something very important

and He couldn't find it. Galo remembered in his dream what he had discovered when he touched his mother's body and so he said to Him: "Touch me, God. This way you will realize that all men are different, then you won't be so sad." But when God was about to touch him, Galo woke up.

He rose to drink a glass of milk and afterwards, despite feeling very cold, he decided to sit down in his chair, next to the bougainvillea.

Sitting in his chair, while the cold made him shiver slightly from the top of his head down to his feet, Galo asked himself if perhaps what the God in his dream was looking for was this house. If so, it seems likely that God was the one who had invented the machine that creates the world's time, he told himself. But if God had invented this great treasure, Galo didn't understand why He hadn't ordered His archangels and celestial armies to protect it.

Following his train of thought, Galo asked himself how God could have lost something so important, although if He had once fallen asleep and then had to go and look for His first-born like a lost sheep, then it was perfectly possible that one night, after sleeping for a long time and with the world being so big, He forgot the place where He had left it, and maybe from that moment onwards He began to search every city in every country; and being so dedicated to the search He had abandoned mankind.

If He was capable of forgetting about His most important work and hadn't even recognized it when He was right on top of it, and if it was for this reason that He had abandoned mankind, then He isn't someone to be trusted, Galo concluded.

Worried, he returned to bed, thinking that maybe one day, in order to defend Amsterdam Street, he was going to have to confront God.

37

═══

"TELL THEM TO GO, Galo, tell them I am very old and that all their racket is going to kill me!" The mother was furious because a week ago construction had begun on a building next to the house, and now her head had begun to hurt.

Galo asked the woman who brought them food from the market every day to get them some roots his mother often used to make a tea that calmed her nerves and eased her pain.

Not long after, a man who said he was Leonardo's father came to pick up the things that his son and Isabel had left behind.

They had rented out the rooms to the construction company that was now making the mother's life impossible. The company set up an office for marketing and sales, not only for the building they were erecting next door but for another four they had already finished in the neighbourhood.

The mother shouted from her bed, and Galo brought her towels drenched in cold water, which she pressed against her neck while she drank her root tea. On the other side of the wall, indifferent to Galo and his mother, the company worked tirelessly.

During one of his routine visits the priest told her to stop playing with witchcraft.

"You need to take medicine and see a doctor who can take away these pains."

"Tell them to leave, Father, to stop their banging, then I'll feel better."

"Don't be silly, Lupe. Progress cannot be brought to a halt because of your migraines," he replied, amused. "Imagine if they paid you any notice, what the world would become? Nothing would ever change. If you were dizzy would you ask the planet to stop spinning, just because it bothered you?"

"They drive me crazy. I wish I could rip my own head off."

"How long have I been telling you to sell, Guadalupe? A few years ago you would have been able to move back to Michoacán. If you had listened to me then and on many other occasions, God would be taking better care of you. In any case you mustn't complain; the opposite, in fact, you should be happy to see how the road looks nicer every day with all these new houses and buildings."

The fact that the priest was happy about what was happening in the neighbourhood worried Galo. Since his dream he had decided to be more vigilant, because if God were to remember that Amsterdam Street was His great treasure then He would definitely tell His army to conquer it, and then He would end up ruling the world. Perhaps these new buildings they were erecting were a sign that something awful was coming.

═══

"Once they demolish this house and build another it will be much harder for my father and Ana to recognize the place," thought Galo as he stood on the roof, watching dozens of builders pounding their mallets and seeing how the iron rods, chunks of cement, and rusty pipes that broke away ended up in a chaotic pile on the ground. Empty trucks would drive in and leave a moment later, carrying enormous quantities of waste. Galo realized that, with every load, they were carrying away a few more of the memories that that house had collected over time, without anyone noticing. And those memories were going to be lost because nobody had taken the time to wrap them in paper and mark them with coloured pencil like he had done with the hair and the moustache trimmings of the men from the Guernica Hairdresser, and if that was happening in the house right next to his then it was very likely that, all along Amsterdam Street, many other demolitions might be going on, destroying its memories forever.

What was the point in demolishing a house just to build another one in the same place if not to erase the memories of the people who lived in it before?

And so Galo thought that what the priest called progress, this force that could not be stopped just because his mother suffered migraines, was in fact a machine, just as important and powerful as the one he looked after, but its purpose was to erase memories so that mankind would forget what had been, or what they had been through, and so they would always have to start from the beginning, and starting from the beginning meant doing the same things all over again.

So, Galo concluded, Amsterdam Street, as well as being the place where true human time was born, was the only tool the world had to use someday in the fight against progress.

The days and months passed, and the men who destroyed the house next door left, and other men built another house on the same spot, and the company eventually sold the new apartments, and the rooms were once again empty, and soon afterwards the owners of the new apartments began to arrive with their furniture and their clothes and their memories arranged in large drawers, and after filling the building that Galo had seen grow over the last few months with their beds and tables and chairs and mirrors and shirts they began to walk along Amsterdam Street over and over again, and the children played with their tricycles and their balls and their bicycles pushing little carts, and the young people sat on the boulevard benches to chat or kiss each other under the lamplight, and the women went to the market and then came back with their bags filled with vegetables or chunks of fish, and sometimes they went and bought a few things from the butcher Mr. Burakov, and the men had to go to Clodomiro Santibáñez's new salon to get their hair cut, and while everyone was doing all these things nobody thought to check what was going on right next to them, in Galo's house. He would sometimes watch them for entire afternoons from the rooftop, still secretly protecting the world's greatest treasure, the treasure that God had lost an eternity ago and that nobody seemed to care about, but that in Galo's opinion was the only chance the world had to stop progress from destroying mankind's memories, because without the memories it would be impossible to be better.

Because everything was the same as always. Thanks to Toño Bermúdez, Galo found out that there were once again more people who had to escape from their houses on foot or on bicycles or on horseback or on buses, because the planes were back in the sky and they were dropping new bombs, despite how much the students that had been Leonardo and Isabel's best friends kept saying that they would change the world any minute now, and all this was happening while his mother, oblivious, slowly began to die, because the doctor who came to see her once the root tea no longer eased her terrible headaches told her that they were not caused by progress and its clamour but by a tumour in the top part of her brain.

═══

One morning they took her away in an ambulance, and that afternoon they brought her back home. The doctors said they were going to treat the headaches with some medicine and that considering her age they didn't recommend surgery. They asked Galo to make sure she always took her medicine on time and said that one of them would come to see her every week.

38

THEY SAY YOU HAVE been dying for a year now, and it looks like you finally did it. I should tell you that some friends of mine and I have been waiting a long time, day after day, for this moment to arrive.

Those who knew how to pray appealed to their saints, those of us who would never step foot in a church, even to spit on a priest, prayed with a good bottle of wine, with every lunch and dinner ever since we arrived in Mexico. But Death, she didn't want to take you so easily. You know, a heart attack would have been enough, cancer, pneumonia, a bullet, because, despite your delusions, you were only human. But it wasn't so; your agony was the longest history can remember, and we have her to thank for that. Don't go thinking I mean your final year, when you kept going and yet not going, I mean the last thirty-six of them. Because you must know that, all modesty aside, your death began when I personally cursed you one afternoon in September 1939, when I swore to heaven and earth that you would die.

Thank you, Death, you were wonderfully cruel to him. Enough to ensure that during those terrible nights of pain and suffering he remembered his victims. How many ghosts populated the twilight of your slow deterioration? Did you recognize

Joseíto Ayala among them? Did you see Adriana's chest, run through with bullets? Did you hear Federico's last poem? While a nun was wiping your asshole after nighttime excretions, did you hear how Esteban Gutiérrez sang before facing his noose? If you didn't, then just you wait, be patient, because you will have plenty of time in eternity to meet them. Over and over again, Francisco, over and over again.

Thank you, life, for offering me this glorious day.

One last thing: rot in hell, Francisco, rot in hell, and I hope the worms eat every last piece of your flesh, and if that god who gave you eighty-two years is listening to this humble atheist, I hope he brings you back to life just to give us the pleasure of seeing you die again.

———

Would they go back? Now that Franco was dead, would they return to Barcelona and Madrid? Would they return to Toledo and Seville? Would they go back and walk the streets of Pamplona and the labyrinthine alleyways of Girona? Would they go back and eat tortillas under the burning sun on the banks of the Duero? Galo remembered the argument between Garfias the poet and Rabbi Cann that had caused so much tension in the Guernica Hairdresser. Was it true that what they had gained in Mexico was more important to those men than the chance to get back what had seemed lost forever? But Galo thought there was a more difficult question to answer: Where does one return to, and who is the person that is returning when thirteen thousand one hundred and forty days have passed between leaving a place and coming back to it? If every single one of those days had a sunrise and a sunset, if on some of them it rained and on others it was cold, if on some they cried and others they fell in love and on others they discovered the taste of a new food, is it possible, then, to return somewhere?

From the rooftop, Galo listened to the speech that Morlans the Catalan read, standing on the second step outside his front door, and he asked himself this and many other questions.

On the rainy morning of the 20th of November, Morlans and his friends had gone out onto Amsterdam Street to shout the same news that Toño Bermúdez had just delivered. They stuck posters they had made by hand on all the posts and benches on the road's central division, inviting to their house whoever wanted to share in the immense joy they were feeling, because at six in the afternoon there would be a ceremony and, most importantly, a party. Their house was across the street from Galo's, less than forty metres away.

Three days ago the municipal government had put up small flags on all the street's ash trees, and to Galo it seemed as though they were not raised, as they were every year, for the anniversary festivities of the Revolution, but that they had instead been put there to help Morlans and everyone else who still lived on Amsterdam Street to celebrate the death of Franco, the man who had forced them to flee Spain, to live in waiting, to live with the feeling that life was happening elsewhere.

The first thing he thought was that from that day onwards Clodomiro Santibáñez would begin to sleep much better because he would no longer dream about cutting off Franco's moustache, because it made no sense at all to cut off a dead man's moustache. But when he began to see all the people who were gathering outside Morlans' house, he asked himself the following questions: How do men feel whatever it is that they feel? What are feelings made of? Memories or the things that have been forgotten? How could the same person feel, at the same time, two things that contradict one another?

Feelings, he thought, are not the same as taste. He had seen people doubt their decision for a moment in the ice cream parlour, but in the end they always made a decision. But it wasn't the same with feelings. And Galo thought this because he remembered that earlier that year he had heard Toño Bermúdez say on the radio that Spanish exiles had been grateful to the president for cutting ties with Franco's government, and that they had gone to his house to thank him and eat with him and applaud him.

Why had they eaten with him and applauded him if they knew that, not long ago, that same man had disappeared and imprisoned people who thought the same way they did? And how could a man who sent those who wanted to start The Revolution to their deaths now organize festivities to commemorate those who had revolted in 1910?

Morlans' Spanish friends were joined later that afternoon by Guatemalans, and the Guatemalans by a few Chileans, all the people who had tried to start The Revolution in their countries and had failed, like the Spaniards had failed before them. And while the president loved them and looked after them and gave them jobs, and while he allowed them to celebrate Franco's death and console themselves over their failed revolutions, and allowed them to imagine that one day they might return and finish what they had started, *here*, thought Galo, that same president had killed, kidnapped, and disappeared all the people who'd wanted to do the same thing. And this was why he remembered Leonardo then; and although it had been seven years since Galo had seen him shout and cry and bleed until they shoved him into a car, he still clearly remembered that Amsterdam Street had seemed deserted that day. Why hadn't Morlans or Garfias or Rabbi Cann or Mr. Lindberg come out of their houses and tried to do something when they could see that seven men were taking Leonardo away? Why had they watched and done nothing, behind the windows of their houses, even after everything that had happened to them?

So, the revolution that had started on the 20th of November, was that The Revolution? And if that had failed, like the one attempted by his only friend, and the ones by the Spanish and the Guatemalans and the Chileans, too, then was it possible for one to ever succeed?

Galo thought about all of this on the day that the man, who had sent Garfias, Santibáñez, Morlans, and so many others to live in Mexico, finally died.

And with these doubts, without knowing whether feelings were made of memories or the things that have been forgotten, he went to bed. His mother, who had been visited by the priest that afternoon, and who had been blind for the past year thanks to the tumour growing inside her head, told him that all those communists who were celebrating that day would, when they died tomorrow, go straight to hell.

Months later, when, on Amsterdam Street there was no trace of the festivities for the Revolution or the party organized by the Spanish for Franco's death, and when Galo left the bedroom at midnight to get a glass of water his mother had asked him for, and when he came back, he discovered she was no longer breathing.

39

I T WASN'T EXACTLY the same, but it was close. The resin was sweeter but less piercing and it didn't fill the patio with a grey cloud. The murmur of the two women praying wasn't the same either, but it was almost like the sound of the saw rising and falling over the wood.

The resin didn't smell the same as the incense, and the prayers did not sound the same as the saw. Galo felt that it wasn't the same, but it was close.

He stopped in front of the casket. The two women whom the priest had brought to take care of everything looked at him for a moment, indifferent, and began to chant the Lord's Prayer again from the beginning.

"If you want," the priest whispered to him, "I can take you tomorrow to the convent to see if they will have you."

"I don't want to."

"You can't stay here alone in the house."

"Yes, I can."

"You are not capable. I already spoke about it with your mother, may she rest in peace."

"If you try to get me out of this house," Galo turned to look at him, "I will kill you."

More frightened by the look on Galo's face than the words he had spoken, the priest left the house followed by the two women, who were not able to finish their prayer.

And so Galo was left alone. He and his mother in her casket. He looked at her again.

"You were right," he said. "Now, you're dead and I am alone. But don't worry. I have many things to do. I have to look after the bougainvillea. I have to sit on the chair my father left me. I have to protect Amsterdam Street. Now you're dead and you don't have to worry about anything."

Do you think . . . What do you think?

Do you feel . . . What do you feel?

Do you dream . . . What do you dream?

———

He asked the couple who had been living in the rooms for the past three months if they could take care of his mother. The night of the wake, out of respect, they had chosen not to come onto the patio, but beforehand they had assured him that they would help him with whatever he needed.

At nine in the morning on April 5, 1976, at age forty-three, Galo received a small box containing what was left of his mother after spending eight hours in a crematory.

He placed the box on the shelf where the only photograph of all three of his family members stood. It was a photo taken in Parque México when he was three years old, next to the bust of General José de San Martín. The father and mother seemed to be smiling. Galo had looked at the camera with his eyes wide open. Now he tried to remember something from that moment, he tried to find a smell, a colour, a feeling in his memory that would merge him with the photographic image, but he couldn't. His life, his true life, the one he could remember, had started the moment he sat down in that chair. It occurred to him that the images saved in a photograph couldn't save memories, and he felt suddenly sad about his mother, who had kept that photo for such a long time.

He walked around the house, visiting every corner. In the kitchen he stopped in front of the table and saw his mother lying down next to Ana's father. In the bathroom he saw old Mr. Gueiser fighting his invisible enemies. He stopped next to the bed he had shared for almost forty years with the body that now fit inside a small box, and he saw the blood of the woman with the blue eyes that had stained the mother's dress. On the patio, he sat on his chair and said to the bougainvillea: "It is only us now."

40

TWO MONTHS AFTER the death of Galo's mother, Martín Benavidez, the tenant from Uruguay, came to find him in the kitchen and told him that he had an idea. He wanted to live in the small room and turn the large one into a dance academy.

"My wife is a dancer, and she can teach people how to tango."

"All right," Galo said. Then asked, "Could the academy be named after Carlos Gardel?"

The couple agreed to this provision, and to celebrate, they had a barbecue on the patio that evening, to which they invited many of their Uruguayan and Argentinean friends. And while the meat was slowly cooking on the blanket of hot coals, some of them sang, accompanied by a guitar: "We learned to love you / from historic heights / where your ferocity's sun / laid siege to death," and others entertained themselves imagining how they would decorate the living room, and then someone put on a record and everyone danced the tango. And Galo, who was happy because he hadn't heard Carlos Gardel since the program had disappeared from the radio but now could listen as often as he liked, Galo, who had been watching how the burning coals beneath the meat slowly dissolved and turned to ash, went without anybody realizing to get the little box in which his mother was and opened it, scattering the powder inside it all over the coals so they could join the ashes being left behind, and the coals eventually consumed themselves until everything was completely extinguished.

When the Gardel Academy was inaugurated and people who wanted to learn how to dance, mostly foreigners, started to meet there, Galo had the feeling that something was beginning again. As he watched them chatting and dancing, he remembered Clodomiro Santibáñez's hairdresser and how the Spaniards and the Jews who came to Amsterdam Street would meet there to feel safe and to talk about the things they were interested in, and now the same thing was happening all over again; but these people came from different places: they were not Spanish, or German, or Ukrainian, but Argentinean, Uruguayan, Brazilian, and Bolivian. They were meeting to discuss very similar things to what he'd overheard in the hairdresser, because they too had had to run away from their town squares and their streets and the shade of the trees they had watched grow, and although they were not talking about Hitler or Franco, they also mentioned armies and dead people and failed revolutions, and Galo realized that the clock that measures the true time of human beings on Amsterdam Street was marking the beginning of a new cycle in history, and that everything, although it was the same, was different and about to start again, and he thought about this until he could almost see, in the middle of the large room, a tall woman, with the sky inside her eyes, waiting for his father to approach her and take her by the waist, and then they began to melt into one another until they became a spinning top, as Gardel sang, "neighbourhood silver plated by the moon, the sound of a milonga is your only fortune."

41

THE PATIO IS DECORATED like an old mansion in the heart of Montevideo. In the eyes of the owners of the Gardel Academy, tonight the bougainvillea is a honeysuckle. They and their students have dressed up like tango dancers from the forties. The men are wearing tight-fitting trousers, grey with black lines, with blue or black jackets, and hats like the one Arturo de Córdova used to wear. The women are wearing silk dresses, with long slits up the sides and high-heeled shoes. Almost all of them have fine shawls draped across their shoulders, because the first nights of April have been brisk. They pushed tables against the walls and turned the middle of the patio into a dance floor. Next to the bathroom is the platform for the small orchestra: a chair for the violinist, two for the guitarists, one in the middle where the bandoneon player will sit, and one step to their right is the microphone the singer will use. It's the Gardel Academy's first anniversary. Galo has taken his chair into his bedroom. He listens to the guests chatting while they wait for the musicians to begin playing. Beneath their voices, like a melancholic and dispassionate rumble, Gardel suggests that the world cares about nothing: it whirls, it whirls. A tall, grey-haired man believes that Che made a mistake, because if he had just stayed here to start the revolution, he wouldn't have ended up betrayed by the communists and dead at the bottom of a Bolivian ravine. "Can you imagine Che," he says, "in Lucio Cabañas's guerilla army? Or what would have happened if instead of meeting Fidel and getting fired up by the 26th of July movement, he had gotten involved with the 23rd of September League? Because if it was just about a date, that wouldn't have made a difference." "It would have failed," says the man sitting next to him, "because the Mexicans would have told him, 'Cool it, you lousy Argentine, don't be so damn cocky,' not like those sweet little Cubans who saw him as some kind of Quetzalcóatl with a beggar's face." An Argentinean says to a Mexican, "To give you an idea, Perón was something like our version of Cárdenas." A Chilean says that Pinochet is on the verge of falling from power and a Spaniard says that he's been saying the same thing for thirty-five years. A Uruguayan insists to his new Bolivian friend that the Tupamaros haven't been defeated. Two Mexicans, sitting apart from everyone else, talk about how the Chileans and Uruguayans are all right, but they can't stand Argentinians, and a woman from Buenos Aires, pressing a cigarette tightly between two fingers as she smokes, whispers to another, who arrived three months ago, that mole isn't bad, but the smell of corn tortillas makes her feel nauseous, and an old Spanish man confesses to two Brazilian women that he is saving what he earns at the university to buy a house in Albacete, because he can't bear the thought of dying here. And while the Spaniards, Argentinians, Mexicans, Brazilians, Chileans, and Uruguayans talk, dozens of glances and smiles cross the patio from one side to the other, far removed from the words their lips utter. A look says, "I love you," another says, "I hate you," another, "Why did you leave me?" another, "If you would like to," another, "I'll die if you don't look at me," and others, which don't seem aimed at anybody in particular, are lost in the air, although they leave the impression of being tied to the leg of a chair or one of the bougainvillea branches, like the look belonging to a young man whose beard is only just starting to grow, which seems to say alone, "I'm so fucking alone, what am I doing in this damn country and what am I going to do tomorrow and the day after and next week, what the fuck am I going to do here all alone?" And Galo, as though he were a ghost through which people's words and glances and smiles could pass without altering their course, wanders around listening and watching, and he realizes that what he discovered at Nueva Michoacán is happening here too, that small things coming out of the blue can change the fate of a conversation, or a look, or a smile, and also that these people's feelings were made both of memories and the things that have been forgotten.

Then the bandoneon maestro sits down and places the instrument on his lap, the violin and the guitars are now ready, the guests fall quiet and stop looking at one another and smiling, because the singer takes the microphone in his hand, closes his eyes and starts to sing the first tango of the evening. "Saint John and old Boedo, and all of heaven . . ." Eight couples stand up from their seats. Sixteen bodies entwine and blend, and Galo, who is standing next to the orchestra, sees that a woman has walked in behind the dancers, through the front door.

He walks over and stops in the middle of the dance floor. The woman who has come in and is standing by the door spots him. She smiles faintly. She walks towards him. The singer says: "South, a light from a store / you will never look at me the way you used to, lying down in the window display, waiting for you."

Galo looks at the eyes looking back at him. Three seconds. The patio has emptied. Galo's eyes and Ana's eyes.

Amsterdam Street has brought her back.

42

D OWNSTAIRS IN THE PATIO, the orchestra was still playing. The couples were dancing, entwining and disentwining arms, legs, looks, and smiles. Upstairs, sitting on the roof, Galo and Ana were talking.

She told him that the three of them lived together in Guadalajara until 1958, when her father decided to accept his sister-in-law's invitation and went to live in New York, but she and her grandfather decided to stay. She told him that Mr. Gueiser died nine years ago, and that just before he did, he asked her to take his body to Berlin, to bury him in a Jewish cemetery, next to his wife. Ana took her grandfather's body to Berlin, buried him, and stayed in the city for one week.

"I went back to Kinkel Street, Galo. But that's not all; while I was there I found my mother. I knew she wasn't dead because once I read letters that my father and my aunt had written one another, and my aunt told him that my mother was very sad and couldn't stop thinking about me. I hated my father for lying to me, and I never forgave him. That's why I didn't go with him to New York. That's why I haven't seen him since.

"I hated my aunt. I hated my grandfather. I hated Berlin. I hated Mexico. I hated my mother. I hated my mother's

German husband. I hated Franz Weill. I hated my body, and I tried to kill myself twice. But then afterwards, I don't know how, I don't know why, I forgave myself.

"I arranged to meet her in a square, two blocks from the train station. I sat down on a bench to wait for her because I had arrived a little early on purpose. I wanted to try and be calm by the time she arrived. A few German children were playing around me, and their mothers were watching them from other benches. They were smiling, Galo. Occasionally they laughed out loud. One of them was pregnant and was knitting. Another flicked through a magazine. One of the children turned too suddenly on his tricycle and fell. He was about to cry but an older girl helped him get up and the boy stopped himself. He didn't want to cry in front of the girl. The mother of the boy who didn't want to cry looked towards the mother of the girl who had helped him and smiled. The other responded with an amused expression. They seemed to understand one another, with no need for more than a smile and a look. The boy got back onto the tricycle and kept going, and the older girl went back to play with her German doll in the sandpit. The cars drove along the roads that surrounded the square and sometimes stopped at the traffic lights. They let other mothers with their children cross the road towards the square. They let others leave the square to go back to their homes.

"I saw a tall, thin woman cross the road, walking along very nervously. The woman was half a metre away from the street when the traffic light turned green, but none of the waiting cars moved. They waited until she reached the sidewalk on the side of the square and then continued on their way. The lady reached the slide and from there looked around the square slowly. She saw the boy on his tricycle, the girl in the sandpit. She saw the mother of the boy, she saw the mother of the girl, and she saw a woman who was reading a newspaper attentively, a woman she did not recognize. She waited. She looked at her watch and waited. Half an hour passed, and she waited. There, standing next to the slide as the children slid down at high speed from the German sky to the ground over and over again, my mother waited.

"If only you had died, mother. If only they really had closed the cemetery so that you couldn't infect anybody. If only a bomb had destroyed your house. If only, mother. You will not hug me, mother, you will not see your Ana, you will not smell her, you will not look at her, you will not cry with her, you will not brush my face with your hand, mother. I will stay here. I will read this German newspaper from top to bottom again and again, and here I will sit while you wait for your daughter to arrive. Because I came in order to not arrive, mother. I came to Berlin to not arrive."

"Do you want me to hug you?" Galo asked.

"Yes."

Galo hugged Ana, and Ana started to kiss him, and Galo kissed each one of her tears. And they wanted to lie down together and embrace one another, so Galo made a mattress using all the small bundles of hair, and they lay on top of them, and they watched how the moon rose in the sky while below, in the patio, the singer said "My beloved Buenos Aires" and a few couples were still dancing and others sang and others waited for a look, or a smile, or a word that had not yet arrived.

She left, after watching the sunrise.

"Goodbye, Galo. I don't know if we will see each other again."

And Galo, who would have liked to tell her about Clodomiro Santibáñez's hairdresser and Cárdenas' moustache, who would have liked to tell her about the homily in which the man whom she had killed went down to the land of the dead to wake up the father who was walking blindly and in rags along Amsterdam Street because he couldn't recognize the house, Galo, who would have liked to tell her about his friend who had ten cats in his lungs, and to her, only to her, he would have read the letters that he had sent, and who would have liked to tell her that last night they lay upon a part of humanity's history, said goodbye to her with his eyes closed and opened them again only once Ana was walking away along Amsterdam Street, oblivious that the time would come when a leaf falling from a tree, or a light breeze would make her realize that everything, from that moment onwards, would be different.

43

THE GARDEL ACADEMY closed at the beginning of autumn of 1982. Martín Benavidez and his wife decided they wanted to return to Uruguay. During the six years it had been open, Galo had rarely been up to the roof, had rarely remembered he was the guardian of Amsterdam Street. He became a taciturn man, and no matter how many times they asked him about the woman who had come to visit him, he never said a word. The truth was his re-encounter with Ana had left him with a sadness that would never abandon him.

Why, he asked himself many times, sitting in his chair, did she not want to stay with me? Why didn't a sudden breeze brush her face, or a leaf fall from a tree at just the right moment? Why did nothing stop her from walking away until I could no longer see her? She will come back. If Amsterdam Street brought her back once, it will bring her again.

But it did not. A year passed and then another and then a third, and Ana did not come back. The street steered thousands of people's destinies, blindly dictated the true human time of the whole world, but it was not capable of bringing her back again.

Where did Ana go when she said goodbye to me? And where does each and every person go, if the road is like a snake biting its own tail? Ana arrived in Berlin to not arrive. She found her mother to not to find her. She came back to my house to not come back.

44

T HESE PLANKS OF WOOD, *these nails that hold them together, they tell my father's story, but looking at the myriad of scratches and dents, I have no way of knowing if he ever reminisced about moments from his childhood or if when he first fell in love he felt the world had changed. If, before he had left, he had taught me the language he used to create, I would know if the legs were made of pine because the smell reminded him of his mother's love, or if the fact that the back tilted towards the floor meant he preferred to see the sunrise with the curtain open just a little, because if he looked at the sun directly he would feel a great melancholy wash over him.*

Every part, every place taken up by that part, every dimension of every one of those parts of the chair where I sat for such a long time is the writing, the words, the full stop or the comma of a book.

I made the decision to translate the chair in order to understand it. I had to write or draw with words something that was my father.

I found several pieces of paper and went to the drawer to look for the pencil with a blue and red end because I thought it would be easier to write about the life of a carpenter that way. The drawer is where my mother always kept the things she considered very important. The things she couldn't live without.

Inside the drawer, along with the pencil, there is a photo of my mother when she was around eight years old, crying and sitting on a stone, and behind her there seems to be a river or something like a river; a letter telling her that my grandmother was very ill and that they thought she wouldn't make it to December, but it doesn't say December of which year; a domino piece with nine black dots, four on one side and after a line that divides it in two, another five dots; a comb missing two teeth; a page from a calendar with the date of the 11th August; and my father's work notebook.

I took out the notebook and read it carefully. There were numbers, measurements, notes to remind himself to buy glue or nails or some tool. All the pages were the same except for the last one: on it he had written *Carlos Gardel* nine times, each one below the next, the first at the top in blue, the second in red, the third in blue, the fourth in red, and so on until the last one.

＝＝

I sat down in front of the chair and looked at it until it got dark. When I wrote the first words, I was thinking about something else. The words came from the blue tip of the pencil while I was thinking about the way my father used to lean against the wall to smoke: his left knee bent so that the sole of his foot could rest against the wall thirty centimetres above the floor, his back still, and his left arm looking as though it were asleep. That's what I was thinking about while I wrote: "I know nothing about my father."

＝＝

Twenty-three days ago I wrote "I know nothing about my father" while I thought about the way he leaned against the wall, and since then I have written nothing, and I don't think I ever will, because this morning I found out that no matter what I do, no matter what I write, I will never know why he wrote Carlos Gardel nine times, switching the colour each time.

45

"I'M TALKING ABOUT Garfias, the crazy poet, the crazy old man who got his hair cut here with you, you told me about him, Galo, the one who used to argue with the rabbi and then cry with him on street corners, and they would get drunk together! The crazy old man, the crazy poet, Clodomiro's friend who taught you that the church was the scum of the earth, he left with a group of friends.

"Can you believe it? At his age, deciding to go off with them to start anew? He bought a bit of land near the hills of Tepoztlán. He bought a few cows and chickens and who knows what else, and he went to start the world all over again.

"They say he got tired of waiting. They say that after what happened to those kids, the ones who lived here in your rooms, the ones they took away, he locked himself in his house and never came out in all those years. He didn't even come out when Morlans the Catalan organized that party to celebrate the death of Franco.

"The crazy old man, the crazy poet! They say one day he finally came out again and said goodbye to his friend the rabbi and sold the house and sold his car, and off he went with three other crazy old poets to that ranch he had bought.

Can you imagine? They say he got tired, and he realized that if the world wasn't changing it was because people didn't want it to change, and so they say he said: 'I'm going to try again, Adam again, Eve again, we are going to find out if it's possible. We are going to see if it's true that there is another way to live. We are going to laugh a little about everything and everyone. We are doing it for all the crazy dead poets who died because they wanted to change the world.' Why don't you go to him, Galo? Why don't you sell this house and go and live with them? Now we are going back to Uruguay because we don't know what else to do, because if one day they threw us out another day we must return and tell them, 'We're back motherfuckers,' and we are going to set the country straight, those military sons of bitches. We are going to sing with Zitarrosa and with Viglietti, we are going to win the elections, we are going to liberate the countryside, we are going to take our loved ones out of prison and raise our dead from their graves so they too can shit on their heads. We are going to shit all over their heads, and we are going to break their balls every day that they have left on this earth, and I don't know if we will be able to change the world, but at the very least they will remember us.

"Go to them, Galo! Go to the old crazy poets! They must invent the world from scratch! Someone has to do it because if not, what will we dream of, Galo, what will we want to do, we who know nothing apart from how to try to change the world!"

════

But Galo, who was listening to his tenant very carefully, picturing thousands of people in a faraway country with little piles of shit on their heads, couldn't decide then and there if he would go or not, because although Amsterdam Street, with its eternal coming and going, had left him without Ana, it did bring him somebody else, forty-three years after he had left. It brought him his father.

46

"I HEARD YOUR MOTHER DIED."

"Yes."

"I am dying too."

"Is that why you're here?"

"I think so."

". . ."

". . ."

"I missed you."

"Me too."

"Why didn't you come back before?"

"I don't know. Why didn't you come looking for me?"

"I couldn't leave the house."

". . ."

". . ."

"Have you been happy?"

"Sometimes. What about you?"

"A little."

"The woman, the one whose hand . . . ?"

"I haven't seen her in thirty years."

". . ."

"Here, I want you have this."

"What am I going to do with a measuring tape?"

"To remember your father by."

". . ."

". . ."

"You were very good. I still use the chair you made me."

"Thank you. And you?"

"I couldn't be a carpenter."

"What are you then?"

"Nothing."

". . ."

". . ."

"Goodbye, son."

The father looked for a moment at the bougainvillea his wife had planted, and then he left, this time forever.

Galo sat down in the chair, and he stayed there until it was afternoon.

47

GALO STAYED SITTING in his chair until it was afternoon. While gazing at the orange measuring tape his father had left behind as a gift, he returned again and again to the image of his father's body that he couldn't get out of his head. He had put on some weight, and there was hardly any hair left on his head. His moustache was gone. There was a scar on his left arm that Galo did not recognize.

When did he hurt his arm, Galo asked himself, and when did he decide to get rid of his moustache, and when did he realize that his hair was falling out to the point of being totally bald? When did he decide that he had been a little happy, and when did he realize that he had no idea why he didn't come to see me sooner? I didn't ask him any of these things, nor did I tell him any of the things that have happened to me that he has no idea about.

And then Galo remembered that when Ana left for the second time, he hadn't told her any of the things he later thought about telling her either.

"Why didn't I tell them, my father and Ana, what I needed to tell them?" Galo asked himself while sitting in his chair, that long afternoon after his father had left forever.

And General Cárdenas didn't tell the Spanish that he had made a mistake in helping them to come to Mexico because he had been thinking about the country inside his head and not the one under his feet. And Franz Weill didn't tell Mr. Gueiser that he was in fact very happy about getting hold of his perfume factory. And Ana's father didn't tell her that her mother was alive and had stayed in Berlin.

None of us, not General Cárdenas, not Mr. Weill, not Ana's father, nor I had said what we needed to say, because that is how men spend their lives: telling themselves things to avoid telling themselves what they really need to hear.

And just like he had discovered that, even though a leaf falling from a tree could change a person's destiny, people still acted as though they knew everything that would happen to them in the future; and that they felt without knowing whether their feelings were made of memories or the things that had been forgotten; and that progress erased memories, and now he realized that words were used to say nothing at all. And if words, Galo thought, don't say what needs to be said, there is no use in speaking, and he made this discovery just a moment before a soft drizzle began to fall on the patio of his house and made him go to bed before eight o'clock in the evening, and just like he had once decided to never leave his house and be nothing and later realized those decisions had been necessary in turning him into the guardian of Amsterdam Street, while he was waiting to fall asleep, he decided he would never speak again.

48

C OULD GALO, who had spent most of his life sitting in a small chair next to a bougainvillea, the guardian, he who would never speak again, leave his house and go with the poet Antonio Garfias to create a new world, like Benavidez had suggested before returning to his country?

Did he now have to make the decision to abandon the small bundles of men's memories?

Could he leave behind the bougainvillea, now that he had seen it grow all the way up to the top of the wall?

His father had come back. Ana had come back. Galo had been there, making sure that the street would allow them to return. He had protected it from dozens of enemies. He had been the one who for days and nights and weeks and weeks and years and years had stayed up all night so that true human time could continue to exist, and despite all of this it had taken them away again and left him all alone.

Had he been right to do this, or was he in fact the one to blame for everything always staying the same? What if it had been his zeal for guardianship that had allowed men to be the way they were? Was it his fault that these things happened? "Could it be my fault," Galo wondered, "that even God was still walking around Amsterdam Street without finding the house where His great treasure was kept?"

If he hadn't guarded it so effectively, would Ana have arrived in Berlin to not arrive? Would his father have come back to not come back?

Had people's lives been better since he decided to become the guardian? Or had everything been worse? Or had everything been the same?

"Staying here served no purpose," thought Galo, "feeding the heart of this great treasure with all the men's memories that I saved from being burned or thrown away served no purpose."

He climbed up to the roof, overwhelmed by his thoughts. The sun was setting. Yesterday's rain had fallen all night long and for some of the following morning, so the bundles underneath the water tank were damp.

How much did these men say to avoid saying anything at all? Galo asked himself. He walked away from the water tank and stood on the edge from which the street could be seen. He watched a girl walking along the street with her mother. A few metres away a man was kneeling down to tie his shoelaces. Two women were talking while carrying bags of vegetables in their hands. Five cars passed in one direction and two in the other. Chapultepec Castle's windows gleamed with the last of the sun's rays.

He remembered, as if time had become a wind that brought images in puffs of air from far away, all the people who had passed through those rooms all those years, one by one. He remembered the foreigners who had arrived and then left again, their hope and also their sadness, pain and nightmares imbued in the walls.

Amsterdam Street, slow, blind, dreary, harsh, like a saw, like a thousand roaring airplanes, like a hundred thousand arms rising and falling, made people repeat their stories over and over again.

And Galo thought that all that time he had been mistaken, that instead of fighting as hard as he had to stop a man or an army or God from invading the street, instead of looking after it with the determination of a child wrapping himself in a flag to jump from the edge of Chapultepec Castle, what he should have done was break it, destroy it, make Amsterdam Street disappear, so that nobody had to come back in order to not come back, as Ana had done, and his father too.

That's why Galo didn't want to leave, because he thought he had to stay to stop the street from continuing to put human beings through the slow torture of having to retrace one's steps over and over again. He wouldn't go to create a new world because his mission, which he knew now was his only true mission, was to destroy the street.

Destroy it so that it could no longer impose so much pain and anguish on humanity, because the street, he thought, had not been able to learn anything after everything that had happened on it, because there the bombers that had filled the air in Europe with ash had flown over it, because there Mr. Lindberg's father and sister had died hanging from the strongest branch of a tree in the Vilna forest, because there they had taken Mr. Gueiser's perfumery away . . .

And if time was born there, then time had to die there too.

And just as he had been its protector, now he must be its destroyer.

Because just like Antonio Garfias had had to go off with his crazy old poets to create a new world so that somebody somewhere could dream once again, Galo had to stop that clock that forced men to walk towards nothing forever, once and for all.

And because he had been thinking all of these things, Galo decided to leave his house for the second time, but this time he would never return. He would leave to walk and walk and walk and never stop, because somebody had to do it, because somebody had to wear down the street until it surrendered and broke, until the stones and the cement and the asphalt split, and until the walls and rooftops that needed to fall fell so that the street could stretch, like an octopus's tentacle, like a whip, towards another place, but never again close in upon itself, the street-snake devouring its own tail.

And it did not matter that the world refused to change despite Garfias and his crazy poets, hidden, silent, stealthy, saying *let's kill burn think sing dance shout but let's do something*, nor that on the street the women kept chatting with the bags of vegetables still in their hands, nor that the girl kept walking with her mother and the man kept tying his shoelaces.

And so Galo decided to be those feet that would forever walk along Amsterdam Street until he defeated it, tired it out, until he turned it into a whip, a stretched-out snake, but first he went up to the roof and packed all the bundles of hair he had been looking after for more than thirty years into a large plastic bag. The hair belonged to Morlans and the rabbi and Garfias and the others, and he tied the bag so that no bundle could fall out and he climbed down with the bag that would accompany him as he walked and walked and walked.

And once he was on the patio, on the 24th of June, 1983, two days before the newspapers would announce the death of the commentator Toño Bermúdez, and forty-eight years after Carlos Gardel boarded a plane to never again step foot on land,

Galo looked at the bougainvillea that he had helped grow year after year, strings and nails and more strings and nails, he looked at the chair that his father had made him so that he would sit and watch him work, so that he would become a carpenter because, if not, he would be nothing . . .

And he reached the front door.

SERGIO SCHMUCLER (1959–2019) was born in Córdoba, Argentina, in 1959 and went into exile in Mexico at the age of seventeen, where he studied social anthropology and screenwriting. His other novels include *La cabeza de Mariano Rosas* and *Detrás del vidrio*. In 2001 he received the Ariel Award from the Mexican Academy of Film for the screenplay of *Crónica de un Desayuno*. As well as a writer of novels, films, and movies, Sergio Schmucler was a tireless fighter for human rights.

JESSIE MENDEZ SAYER is a literary translator and editor currently based in Mexico City. She studied history and Spanish at the University of Edinburgh. She cut her teeth in the publishing world at Editorial Anagrama in Barcelona before returning to London to work as a literary scout, with a particular focus on contemporary Spanish and Latin American literature. She moved to Mexico City in 2017, where she works as a translator. Her literary translations include books by authors such as Guillermo Arriaga, Alonso Cueto, and Alberto Barrera-Tyzka.